# AND BY GOD'S HAND YOU SHALL DIE

DAVID SODERGREN

*Fulci lives!*

# PART I

LIFE

# 1

1972

On the night the Manhattan Riverfront Church burned down, Father Patrick Morgan killed for the first time.

The murders weren't planned. They weren't premeditated.

They were a crime of passion.

For on that miserable night, when the fires blazed high and the aisles of the church ran red with blood, Father Patrick Morgan killed for the only being he had ever loved, and the only being who had ever loved *him*.

His God.

It began on a rainy Tuesday evening.

The blank moon had vanished behind a bank of storm clouds when Father Patrick left the grim confines of his small apartment and stepped out onto the street. The rain didn't bother him. It was penance for his sins, soaking through his cassock and weighing him down. All around, the dregs of society ambled past him, a never-ending ballet of bodies dodging and colliding with each other, sometimes by accident, sometimes deliberately. They were *all* out tonight. The hustlers, the junkies, the pimps. The crepuscular twilight people, vampires who fed on the souls of their victims rather than their blood. Few paid him any attention as he strode by in his cassock. Even the hookers figured a priest wasn't worth their time.

He eyeballed them as he walked. Two women in short skirts and fishnet stockings huddled in a doorway to avoid the downpour, while a man in a brown trench coat fiddled with himself behind a trash can, the lights from passing cars illuminating him like a ghost.

LIVE NUDE GIRLS promised one store, the letters lit up in lascivious red that seemed to bleed from the building. Father Patrick snorted. Of course it was red. The color of *sinfulness.* How appropriate for New York City, the most degenerate place in the world.

A movie theater advertised a double bill of ASYLUM OF SATAN and BLOOD FREAK. The poster beneath the marquee was for something called TEENAGE SEX KITTEN, in 'undulating color.' A bored-looking girl sat at the box office flicking through a magazine, only glancing up when a man slapped a crumpled dollar on the counter. The girl sneered at him with a mouthful of gum and slipped him a ticket.

"Enjoy the show," she said.

Father Patrick shuddered. What had become of the world? When had this new licentious age first dawned?

A police cruiser rolled past, fat raindrops beating against the hood. The cop's arm rested out the window, a cigarette burning between his fingers. What chance did the children stand if their role models demonstrated illicit behavior?

Father Patrick could take no more. He peeled off the street and left the loathsome cesspit of 42nd Street like he was waking from a bad dream. A bum called after him, dirty digits grasping at his cassock.

"May God have mercy on your soul," said Father Patrick under his breath as he shoved the man aside. The bum clattered into a trash can, knocking it over.

"Fucking asshole," muttered the bum, but Patrick was already long gone.

He wiped the rain from his eyes and said a prayer. Traffic thrummed around him, music blaring from the radio of a street gang.

"Hey Padre, you got a dime?" someone shouted.

The priest took a right turn, heading along the Hudson, his sodden shoes squelching underfoot. It was quieter here. A young woman with mousy brown hair and glasses emerged from the shadows of a doorway and bumped into him.

"Pardon me," smiled Father Patrick.

The woman glared at him. "You fucking blind, asshole?" She clutched a paper bag to her chest. Patrick looked at the store she had exited.

BIG AL'S ER TIC BO KS, read the sign. It didn't take a scholar to figure out the missing letters.

He shook his head. Even the women were using the dirty stores now. Even the *women*. He supposed it shouldn't come as a shock. Women were the great corrupters, after all. It had started with the temptation of Eve, and continued to this day. He stared at the woman as she walked away. Her shorts were so small he could see the lower curves of her buttocks.

"You're going to hell," he shouted.

"Go suck a dick, Father," she called back.

He sighed and turned away. "Forgive her. She knows not what she does."

Father Patrick walked on. There was only one place he wanted to be right now. His church. His *true* home. The rain was easing up, leaving deep puddles that reflected the store signs and passing headlamps. Soon, even they disappeared, and Father Patrick found himself standing before the Manhattan Riverfront Church.

It was a beautiful sight. The church loomed over him, and he basked in its heavenly glory. It filled him with God's warmth. He gazed up at the spire, almost invisible against the black sky, and raised his arms towards—

A light came on.

A light inside the chapel, shining through the stained glass window like a beacon.

Father Patrick's heart quickened. A sign from God? A smile crossed his lips, then faded. No. More likely *trespassers*. Thieves, or junkies breaking in for a quiet place to do… whatever it was they did. He stalked towards the gate, rummaging in his pockets for the keys to the padlock. He always carried them with him, never daring to leave them in his apartment, what with the broken lock and the strange people mingling in the halls and the hoodlums next door fornicating unashamedly, their headboard thudding against Patrick's wall as he prayed for God to strike them down mid-coitus.

The padlock opened and Father Patrick swept through the gate. The light had gone off again, but he knew they were in there. He had seen them.

Deciding against using the main entrance, he instead hastened around to the side door. As he carefully stepped inside, Father Patrick was unafraid, for he had the Lord on his side.

The door led into a store room. Patrick knew it well. It was far from the first time he had entered the church by the side entrance. The *quiet* entrance. He often came here at night to reflect, keeping the lights off so as not to attract unwanted attention.

He left the store room, entering a darkened hallway and passing the door to the basement. Those fools. If they had gone down *there,* he would never have known.

The sacristy was next. His trailing hand brushed along the door frame, and he paused, listening.

A voice drifted ethereally through the empty, black corridor.

A woman's voice.

*Of course.*

The temptress.

The *whore.*

He moved like a shadow towards the area of worship, his fingers fidgeting above the handle as he pressed his ear to the vast oak door.

They were fornicating. He heard the vile smack of their flesh, the tortured panting and moaning. He grasped the handle, then stopped himself, an idea forming in the dank recesses of his mind. Turning away from the door, he retreated to the small kitchen area. Wearing the darkness like a cloak, he slid silently towards the washing basin and pulled open a drawer, his hands raking through cutlery until they came to—

"Ah!" he cried, as his fingers found the sharp edge of the knife. He lifted it by the handle, listening to the quiet drip of his blood onto the linoleum floor.

The knife felt good in his hand.

He gripped it with holy fervor as he left the kitchen, arriving once more at the chapel door. He opened it soundlessly, though it wouldn't have mattered. The man and the woman inside were making enough noise to wake the dead.

*"That's it, baby,"* the man said. *"Fuck me hard."*

Patrick imagined the long-deceased denizens of the churchyard hammering on their coffin lids in horrified frustration. His fist trembled.

*"Hurry up,"* grunted the woman. *"We could get arrested for this."*

*"That's why I paid you extra."*

The vibrations extended to the rest of Patrick's limbs. God's righteous rage flowed through him. He saw them now.

The desecrators.

They were by the pulpit, flanked by several lit candles. The man had his back to him, his pants and underwear bunched up around his ankles. His hairy posterior pumped against the woman, her own buttocks slapping rhythmically against the pulpit.

Prostitution. Prostitution in God's house!

The woman's spread legs protruded from the man's sides. She leaned back, extending her arms wide in an unconscious imitation of the crucifix that hung above her, and for an instant, the pair resembled a grotesque humanoid spider.

Patrick started towards them, his robes swishing across the carpet.

*"Stop,"* said the woman.

Patrick froze.

The man didn't. *"What's the matter now?"*

*"I heard something."*

*"Bullshit. There's no one else here. Now shut up and let me finish."*

*"Shit, I always get the ones into the freaky shit,"* sighed the woman, a wry smile crossing her lips at the exact moment Father Patrick Morgan stepped out of the darkness and thrust his knife between the man's shoulders. The sinner jerked violently as Patrick wrenched the weapon free. Blood jetted from the wound.

The whore looked at Patrick, her eyes widening until they resembled two icy planets. Her mouth dropped open, but no sound came out. Patrick rammed the knife into the man again. The body stiffened. Blood poured down the man's spine and pooled on the carpet. Patrick withdrew the knife. With his free hand, he took the man by his hair and yanked his head back. The edge of the blade scraped against the exposed jugular while the woman looked on, the devil's whore gazing upon her foul handiwork, foolish and uncomprehending.

Patrick slit the man's throat. The flesh tore like cheap fabric, thick gouts of dark blood gushing forth and spraying wildly over the pulpit. The man gurgled, then dropped lifelessly to his knees, exposing the woman in all her naked glory. She didn't even try to cover herself, her breasts stained red with the man's lifeblood.

Only now did she seem to understand.

"This is God's house," said Patrick. He raised the knife. It caught the light of the candles, the blood glistening. "And you shall not defile it!"

The woman did not scream as he expected. Instead, she shoved Patrick, barging past him and running for the exit. She might even have made it, had he not reflexively extended a foot and tripped her. Patrick heard the dull thud of her hitting the ground. In the dim glow of the candlelight, he watched her pale, nude body as she tried to rise.

"Help!" she screamed.

Patrick stalked towards her. *"But among you there must not be even a hint of sexual immorality, or of any kind of impurity, or of greed, because these are improper for God's holy people."* He wiped the bloody knife against his cassock. "Ephesians, 5:3."

He never noticed the candle lying on its side by the pulpit, burning softly. He never noticed it roll across the shelf towards the fabric banner that read JESUS IS LIFE, hand-stitched by a deeply pious member of the congregation.

And he certainly never noticed the banner catch fire.

Under different circumstances, he might have done, but now the woman had turned onto her back and was pleading with him as she kicked her way across the well-trodden carpet, her legs spread wide open. Patrick gazed at the dark patch between her thighs, the root of all the world's evils, and clenched his fist around the handle of the knife.

"Leave me alone," sobbed the woman.

*"I will be grieved over many who have sinned earlier and have not repented of the impurity, sexual sin and debauchery in which they have indulged."*

He was closing in on her.

"Corinthians, 12:21," he said.

She managed to stand, stumbling away from him towards the door. He was surprised how clearly he could see her.

"God's holy light guides me," he whispered, as his shadow danced and flickered across the wall. The woman grabbed a bible from a pew and hurled it towards him. It struck his chest painlessly. Patrick could feel nothing right now, nothing except virtuous power flooding his veins, the warm breath of God carrying him onwards. The woman reached the door. She fumbled with the handle, shrieking and crying.

"Tremble before God," said Patrick. "Tremble naked before him, and repent!"

She turned to him one last time. "Fuck your God!" she screamed, and then she flung open the door.

Patrick leaped forwards, stomping his heel on the back of her ankle. A bone snapped loudly, and the woman dropped to the floor. Her leg was bent at an absurd angle, white bone jutting from torn skin. She spluttered a mouthful of blood as Patrick kneeled by her.

"It's not too late," he said, stroking a hand through her bloodstained hair. "There's still time to beg for forgiveness."

"Please," said the woman, shaking her head, her eyes rimmed with crimson tears. Patrick gazed benevolently down at her. Such a waste of a pretty girl. Breathing heavily, he caressed her face, running his hand down her neck, then further, *further,* to her breasts. He stared at them, at *her,* as he felt that familiar stirring in his groin. He ran his hand over the curve of one breast, his fingers catching on the soft bud of her nipple, then down her stomach towards—

"No!" he roared. "You shall not tempt me, jezebel!"

He averted his eyes from her ugly nakedness, her wicked body, unprepared for the woman to punch him square in the jaw. Patrick's head rocked back, the knife dropping from his hand. When he looked around, the woman was crawling towards the exit, dragging her ruined leg behind her like a useless sack of garbage.

Patrick watched as she scrambled through the exit on her hands and knees. He swung his hand between her legs, his fingers sinking into the wet flesh of her sinful hole, and dragged her backwards until her head rested against the doorframe. Then he took the door and slammed it shut.

Her skull cracked. The woman's body spasmed upon impact. She fell flat, her shoulders jerking. Patrick opened the door, slamming it once more. This time, the skull shattered. The door closed fully, savagely bisecting the whore's head. Blood fountained from the ruined appendage as her body twitched. Patrick watched the jiggle of her buttocks in horrified fascination, then shut his eyes before she could entice him further with her blasphemous flesh.

He put his fingers to his nostrils, fingers that had been inside her, and inhaled her foul, female scent.

Sweat dripped down the nape of his neck. It was hot... so *hot*. The fires of hell were surely burning, welcoming the filthy harlot to an eternity of damnation. He smiled to himself, imagining what abhorrent tools the devil would use to fill the woman's orifices, then twisted his neck to gaze at the pulpit. The smiled melted from his face.

The pulpit was ablaze. The whole church was, from the pews to the curtains. Holy water bubbled in the font, boiling over as flames licked the walls, reaching the great wooden crucifix above the pulpit. It caught fire as the stained glass window exploded from the heat, raining sizzling hot glass down over the rows of pews. Was it Patrick's imagination, or did the thin wooden Jesus affixed to the cross cry out in torment as the flames reached him, burning his lily white skin a deep charcoal black?

"My church!" cried Patrick.

The crucifix leaned forwards, tearing itself free from the wall. It hung there, ablaze, and then toppled onto the pulpit. Patrick ran towards the inferno, the heat stinging his eyes. The cross burned within, and he plunged his hands into the flames, grasping the wood and lifting the crucifix, placing it upon his back before Hell could claim the idol as its own. It burned quickly through his cassock. Patrick roared in agony and stumbled down the aisle. His clothes caught fire, the flames rising, burning his skin, his hair, the acrid stench of melting flesh infiltrating his nasal cavities.

As Patrick carried his savior upon his shoulders, he prayed to God. He prayed not for an end to his own suffering, or for his salvation. Instead, he prayed for a lifetime of violence and bloodshed for the sinners and the temptresses that had taken over the world.

If he had to die to prove his purity, then so be it.

After all, a bit of suffering never hurt anyone.

The church burned for seven days and seven nights. No matter how much water the firefighters doused it with, they could not control the blaze. Every time it appeared the battle was over, another flame would erupt from out of nowhere like weeds in a garden.

Then, at midnight on the seventh day, the fire abruptly ceased. The firefighters looked at each other in confusion, unsure of what they had done. It was as if someone had simply turned the gas off. They searched the rubble, more out of duty than belief. No one could have survived an inferno like that, they all agreed.

But they were wrong.

It was a young man named Elroy Wallace who found it. A staircase, buried beneath debris and ash and charred wood, that led down to a basement. It was agreed that the area was too dangerous to investigate, until Elroy heard the soft sounds of quiet sobbing coming from down the stairs. Two volunteers descended the crumbling wooden steps that night.

What they found was impossible, they knew, and yet their eyes told them otherwise.

The interior of the basement appeared to have been unmarred by the fire. There were no burns, no scorch marks, no smoke damage. It was as if the area had been somehow... protected.

The sobs grew louder, and the men followed until they found the source.

A man, naked and horribly burned, lay atop a crucifix, his arms wrapped around a withered and blackened carving of Jesus.

When he saw his rescuers, he looked into Elroy's eyes and smiled a lipless, charred grimace.

"It's a miracle," whispered Father Patrick.

## 2

———————



The assholes were waiting.

Candy — or Mary Holmes, to her friends and family back home — sighed as she spotted the protestors gathered outside her place of work. There were a lot of them tonight, so she hung back, leaning against the closed-down grocery store on the corner, and finished her smoke, steeling herself to face them. It was seven-thirty, and she knew from experience they wouldn't disperse until nine at the earliest.

They were always there, with their chants and their signs, every day since she started one year ago in the frigid winter of 1980. Sometimes there were as many as fifteen of them, occasionally as few as two, but the group was always present in some form, and always led by their venerable leader, Father Patrick Morgan.

She glanced at the throng of perpetually outraged citizens — there must have been close to twenty of them today, the most she had ever seen — but couldn't locate the priest. It wasn't like he was difficult to spot. The man was well over six feet tall, and scar tissue covered his face and hands.

*Maybe he finally found something better to do with his time?*

Candy half-smiled. The ghoulish old bastard was probably out protesting abortion clinics instead. Some men are only happy when they're harassing women.

She checked her watch. Her shift had officially started five minutes ago.

"Dammit."

She ground her cigarette against the boarded-up store window and walked towards the group. One of them spotted her coming, a thin man with a combover and neatly trimmed mustache.

"The devil's concubine approaches!" he shouted. With military precision, the protestors formed a wall, blocking the entrance and raising their placards above their heads in unison.

DOWN WITH VICE, read one.

SAY NO TO SLUTS, read another.

And there, inevitably, was WON'T SOMEBODY THINK OF THE CHILDREN?

That slogan always made Candy laugh. The ultimate get-out clause for anyone whose delicate sensibilities had been offended.

*It's not the children you have to worry about,* she thought. *In a place like this, it's their fathers who're the troublemakers.*

"Whore!" shouted one of the protestors, a surly woman in faded denim jeans and a brown overcoat. The word wiped the smile from Candy's face.

*Don't engage, don't engage.*

"This used to be a family-friendly neighborhood!"

She had heard it all before. Candy's place of work, the

building they had pinpointed as the source of all the nation's ills, was a brothel. That was bad enough for Father Patrick and his devout followers, but what really galled them was that it had once been a church.

The story was part of New York legend. Apparently, when the holy edifice burned down nearly a decade ago, some cowboy developer had bought the land with the intention of building a small factory. That the notorious cheapskate managed to complete construction came as a surprise to many. That the builders — in apparent protest at their poor pay and lack of sanitary working conditions — neglected to put any windows in, came as rather *less* of a shock.

Reportedly, the genius behind the project was quoted as saying, "The only use for a windowless building is a goddam whorehouse," words which had rung in the ears of a newly widowed woman by the name of Martha Stevenson. Martha, finding herself wealthy and free for the first time in her life, had promptly snapped up the four-storey monstrosity for a song, and turned it into precisely that.

A whorehouse.

Candy and at least a dozen other girls worked there, and worked damn hard, so she was in no mood for anyone's judgement today, especially judgement handed down from rich suburban moms who never had to worry about where the next rent check was coming from.

"You should be ashamed of yourself," said one woman. "You're a filthy whore!" She spat at Candy as she approached, the glob landing in front of her feet, and continued her vitriolic outburst. "Your sinful building rests on sacred land. That's a holy place you're entering!"

Candy kept her head down, her backpack hanging from

one shoulder. "Yeah, I know all about people entering holy places, thank you."

The protestors — and what an ugly, dreary lot they were — linked arms, forming an impenetrable semi-circle around the double door entrance.

"Excuse me," said Candy, trying to remain calm. "I need to go to work."

A beige man in a beige coat and beige slacks shook his head resolutely. "Not tonight. Go home and repent. Pray to God to forgive your sins. Ask that he cleanse your—"

"My what?" snapped Candy. "My cunt?"

The man shrank back in horror, the color draining from his face. A couple of the women gasped.

"Your *soul!*" the man shrieked. "Get on your knees and beg for forgiveness before it's too late!"

Candy shook her head. She would be on her knees tonight for sure, albeit for very different reasons.

"I don't have time for this," she said, turning from the group and striding down the alleyway by the side of the building. There was another entrance there, and though it would make her even later for her shift, it was better than conversing any further with those morons. She told herself they were harmless, but the problem with religious crazies was that she was never sure how far they were willing to go in support of their so-called forgiving beliefs.

The wind swirled through the alley. Fall had passed by, and winter was making its presence known. She hugged her arms across her chest.

"Just one more year," she said to herself. One more year, and then she would graduate from business school and be free from this city, free from her cramped apartment, and free from Father Patrick and his flock of psychos.

The alley was dark, cloaked in shadow from the neighboring building. A distant foghorn from a boat on the Hudson drowned out the chants and shouts of the protestors, the click of her heels echoing off the graffiti-coated walls as she deftly dodged the... wait, what *was* that? She paused, looking down at the small, mangled body that lay at her feet. In the semi-darkness, she couldn't tell what it was... or had once been. A fox? A cat? She averted her eyes and moved to step around it, then froze.

There was a new sound. A gentle swishing across the ground. Were the protestors following her? She glanced over her shoulder, wishing she hadn't come this way alone. The main road seemed oddly far away, but no one was there. No one she could see, anyway.

A chill breath ran the length of Candy's spine.

"Is someone there?" she called, as the sound whispered through the alley like billowing curtains brushing against the carpet in a gothic mansion.

There was no reply.

She willed her legs to carry her onwards, heading for the back door. Dammit, she resented the way those people made her feel. It was *her* body, and she could do with it what she damn well pleased. And if that meant selling it for sex to pay her way through college, then that was *her* choice. There were worse jobs out there. The work was easy, the clients mostly pretty easy-going. The pay wasn't great once Martha took her cut, but the tips were ten times what she had made waitressing.

As Candy arrived at the back door, a thought struck her. What if it was locked? They usually kept it unlocked so that certain high-profile clients could make a surreptitious exit. But not always...

She approached, smiling to herself as she noticed the

thin sliver of light where the door was propped open. If she hurried, Martha might never know she was late.

The swishing sound again. Closer this time.

Much closer.

Candy reached the door, grasping in the darkness for the handle.

"*Whore.*"

She shouldn't have turned. At the sound of the voice, she should have rushed straight inside. But it was surprise, more than anything, that made Candy look back to see the figure looming out of the shadows in his black cassock.

"Wretched, obscene whore!" croaked Father Patrick, his wizened face pulled taut into a ball of righteous anger

Candy couldn't help herself.

She screamed.

The priest came for her. He grabbed her forearm and hauled her towards him.

"Hey," said Candy, "Let go!"

"Foul, filthy pervert!" He gripped her tightly. She tried to shake free, but his fingernails had hooked into the thin material of her sweater. His eyes were blank, glazed over, the purple flesh around them sagging like melted wax.

"Get your fucking hands off me," she said, her heart pounding.

The priest shook her violently, speaking as if in a trance. "You sell your bodies on sacred land. You spread your repulsive legs in God's holy temple."

His claws dug in further.

"Infidel!" he cried, as she attempted to prise up his crooked fingers, his skin cold to the touch, like raw chicken, but hard and bony. "You will stand naked before the Lord and face your judgement!"

Candy felt his ragged nails penetrate her skin.

"Get the fuck off me!"

He wasn't listening. Spittle flew from his lipless mouth as he spoke. "You shall stand naked before the Lord and receive a punishment *fit for a whore!*"

His other hand found her neck, pressing her up against the wall, into the shadows. To the outside observer, she was gone, vanished into inky oblivion.

"This is a holy place!" shrieked Father Patrick.

"Fuck you!" screamed Candy, and thrust her knee between his legs. The priest doubled over, gasping out a reedy wheeze. Candy shoved him, and he fell to the ground, gazing up at her with gray eyes that narrowed to slits.

"I'm sorry," said Candy. Apologizing was all she could think to do. Tears sprang to her eyes, tears of pain and anger and frustration. "Just leave me the fuck alone!"

"Charlatan!" he hissed, and started to rise.

She wrenched the door handle down, kicked away the ratty old sneaker that had propped the barrier open, and slammed it shut with a satisfying metallic *clang*. The key was in the lock, and she turned it until the deadbolt thudded into place. Only then did she allow herself to lean back against the cold metal and close her eyes.

Suddenly fists pounded against the door. Candy screamed and threw herself against the wall as the priest continued roaring his apocalyptic pronouncements.

*"Whore! Filthy perverted whore! The end of the world approaches, and the sinners shall be swept away in a purifying sea of blood!"*

"Fuck you," she whispered, double-checking that the door was locked. She would have to tell Martha and the other girls about this. Though the priest had threatened them before, and tried to intimidate them with his impotent tantrums, this was the first time he had resorted to actual violence.

Taking a deep breath, she turned away and started down the dark, cobwebbed corridor that led to the reception area, wondering why the fuck *she* had been the one apologizing. That old bastard had assaulted her. A needling pain in her arm drew her attention to a wet stain on her sleeve where the priest's rancid nails had cut her.

*Damn it.*

She couldn't afford a new sweater. Hell, she doubted she could afford a laundry bill, what with rent due next week.

"It's gonna be okay." She wiped her eyes. "Everything's gonna be just fine."

She had to relax, had to look presentable. She was late, and doubtlessly had a client waiting for her. Puffy eyes and mascara tears were not what her regulars paid her for. It was her job to be the most beautiful women they would ever sleep with, someone to make their most decadent, intimate fantasies come true, to inject some erotic excitement into their otherwise humdrum lives.

And she was damn good at it.

She rolled up her sleeve and tried to inspect the damage, but it was too dark. Blood dripped from her wrist onto the floor, the steady patter sounding like footsteps. It made her uneasy, so she cupped her hand over the wound to stop the noise. Warm blood oozed into her palm, and yet... the faint sound of ponderous footsteps continued. She glanced nervously down the corridor.

The steps were getting louder. She looked to her right with dreadful certainty, her eyes falling on the basement door. The sounds were coming from behind it.

Someone was climbing the stairs.

Candy turned from the door and resumed her journey.

"Not tonight, bitch," she muttered. "Not tonight."

As she walked, she could have sworn she heard a soft scratching from the basement. She quickened her pace.

*Probably rats. Just plain old giant New York rats.*

She never looked back. Not when the scratching became more frantic, or even when the handle started to turn. And by the time the basement door creaked fully open on ancient hinges, there was no one around to hear it.

**3**

———

When Candy entered the reception area, Martha was waiting for her with a dog-eared paperback resting on her lap.

"You're late," she said without looking up. The older woman's hair was pulled back into a tight ponytail that draped over the shoulder of her chiffon gown, and she held her latest affectation, a wide paper fan she had brought over from a recent trip to Hong Kong.

"The protestors," said Candy. "They wouldn't let me in."

Martha scowled. "It's the same every night. You should be used to it. Why didn't you use the back door?"

"I did." She held up her bleeding arm for Martha to see.

"The priest do that?"

Candy nodded.

Martha seemed unimpressed. "Well, get yourself cleaned up. You've a client waiting in room twelve. If you're not there in ten minutes, you're not getting paid."

"But—"

"This isn't a charity, girl. Stop sniveling, go shower, and

change into something... sexier. You look like you're delivering girl scout cookies."

There was no point arguing with Martha, not when she was in one of her moods. As far as bosses went, she wasn't the worst Candy had worked for. The rumor was that she had killed her husband to inherit his money, but brothels were as bad as offices and schoolyards for gossip, so Candy took everything she heard with a grain of salt.

Martha picked up her paperback and pretended to read it. "Nine minutes."

With her bag slung over her shoulder, Candy jogged towards the beaded curtain that led into the girls' private locker room. The dingy area was lit by a single bulb that hung unconvincingly from a frayed and yellowing cord. Purple lamé pants and a brown suede waistcoat lay crudely folded on a side cabinet.

"Foxy, you in here?" called Candy.

*"In the shower,"* came the muffled reply.

Candy smiled. She knew it would be Foxy. None of the other girls could pull off that look. Candy took fishnet stockings, a fuchsia leather skirt, and a gold metal mesh top from her bag. She quickly stripped, stuffed her civilian clothes into the bag, and checked her arm. There were three thin cuts from where the priest had grabbed her. It was nothing. The marks would be gone in a week.

She padded naked into the shower block, where the factory workers would have cleaned themselves off after a hard day's work, had the factory ever opened. Instead, beautiful women now used the showers to wash cum off their tits and out of their pussies. What would the workers have made of *that*, Candy wondered with a grin?

Foxy — Candy didn't know her real name, only that she had borrowed her current moniker from a Pam Grier movie

— was showering, standing back so as not to wet her immaculately coiffured hair.

"How do you do it?" asked Candy as she pressed the button and stepped aside to avoid the freezing jet of water that burst from the nozzle.

Foxy turned to her, foamy suds running down her legs. "Do what?"

"Keep your hair like that? After my first client, I usually look like I've fallen out of a tree."

"Oh, that's easy. I have one rule, and one rule only. They're not allowed to touch my damn hair."

Candy laughed, putting her hand into the water to see if it had heated up. It hadn't, but time was of the essence, so she braced herself and stepped into the jet.

"Jesus Christ," she shuddered, her body clenching in protest. She grabbed a thinning bar of soap and scrubbed at the red marks on her arm.

"Hey. When did you start using?" asked Foxy.

It took Candy a moment to understand. Foxy was staring at the puncture wounds in the crook of her elbow.

"Oh, no, it's not that. The priest hooked his claws into me outside."

Foxy let out a breath. "Good. I mean, not good that the wacko hurt you, but you know that if you ever start using, I'm gonna beat your ass, right?"

Candy smiled. "I know you would. Though that doesn't sound too bad, actually."

Foxy laughed and smacked Candy across her wet rear. The slap echoed through the shower block. "That's as close as you'll ever get to me, girl. I'm man only."

"Thought your only rule was don't touch the hair?" teased Candy.

A sly smile spread across Foxy's face. She pulled Candy

into a gentle embrace, their nude bodies pressing against each other. Foxy's hands slid down to the small of Candy's back, then further, her hands finding her ass.

"Well," she said, "If you ever want to hire me, you know where to find me." She burst out laughing, and Candy playfully shoved her.

"You're such a bitch," she laughed. Though she knew Foxy was just fooling around, part of her — the part that made her knees go weak and her heart race and her thighs tingle — wondered what it would be like to spend an evening with Foxy.

*Yeah, great idea. You can't afford your rent, but you can pay for sex with your co-worker.*

Ah well, it was a fantasy. It would give her something to think about that night as she shuddered in make-believe ecstasy beneath some poor client.

"You coming?" asked Foxy.

Candy felt herself blush. "What? No! I'm just, I was just thinking—"

"I meant, are you coming with me, or are you just gonna stand under that cold water all night?"

"Oh, yeah," said Candy. "That's what I, uh, thought you meant."

"Yeah, sure." Foxy tossed a towel at her. "Here, use this to hide your blushes."

Shivering, Candy dried herself off. Due to the building's lack of windows, the air con ran at full blast all day and night. She glanced up at the grate, at the thick threads of dust blowing at an angle from the metal bars. Well, at least it was an incentive to get dressed quicker.

She joined Foxy by the fingerprint-smeared mirror, hurriedly applying lipstick and mascara.

"Dunno why we even bother," said Foxy. She sprayed a

blast of cheap perfume on her neck and breasts. "Half the time they don't even look at your face."

"Tell me about it," said Candy. She touched her finger to her nose, running it over a small bump. A zit. Great, just what she needed. Well, there was no time to deal with it. She brushed her hair and slipped into her panties, not bothering with a bra. Her john last night had taken so long to get it off he lost his erection. No, a bra was too much admin for most married men.

Get them in and get them out, that was Martha's unintentionally euphemistic policy.

"How's college going?" asked Foxy, as she pouted at herself in the mirror.

"Good." She fastened her skirt, tugging the hem down over her ass. "Been a tough semester, but rewarding. Not long now."

"Then you're outta here, right?"

"Well, I'll need to find a job first. What about you?"

Foxy shrugged. "Guess I can't do *this* forever. I'm twenty-eight already."

Candy nodded in understanding. Prostitution was a young person's game, and for many clients, Foxy was past her prime at twenty-eight.

"Hey, when I open my own business, you can come work with me."

"Don't you mean *for* you?"

Candy shook her head. "No. We can be partners. You know fashion better than anyone. If I'm opening a boutique, I want someone like you by my side."

Foxy half-smiled. "You're sweet. But you'll move on and forget about this place. And that's okay. That's for the best. You've got a bright future, I can tell. You're smart and beautiful." She broke into a grin. "A dangerous combination."

"I won't forget you, Foxy."

"That's because you're in love with me."

The beaded curtain jangled as someone entered. Candy turned to see a slender girl in blue cut-offs and a tight gray tee with ANGEL IS INNOCENT printed on the front.

Linda. She lit a cigarette and looked at Candy. "Martha said I was to tell you *one minute*. I don't know why."

"I do," said Candy. She stood. "Guess I'd better go spread my legs for the good of all mankind."

4

---

CANDY'S FIRST JOHN OF THE NIGHT WAS ONE OF HER REGULARS, a burly gentleman who hid behind the decidedly unoriginal nom de plume of John Smith. His lack of imagination extended to his bedroom antics, where he enjoyed the missionary position and manhandling her boobs. He was pleasant enough, and offered some cautious small-talk afterwards while he dressed, which always amused Candy. He asked about her life, and how college was going, and she told him it was fine and asked about his kids, a subject she knew he enjoyed talking about. It paid off. He left her a twenty-dollar tip.

Afterwards, Candy cleaned herself in the washroom, shuddering at the freezing water she ladled from a bucket. She dressed, and tucked the bill into her panties where Martha wouldn't see it.

A little small-talk went a long way with some of those poor saps. A lot of them were men who were lonely. They reminded her of the old people that would come into the diner where she had worked the previous year. They just wanted to talk to someone, to forge some kind of human connection. Lost souls flitting through life, struggling to make sense of it. She supposed she was no different. Next year she would graduate, and the thought terrified her. What then? What would she do with her life? At least in here, she knew what she was doing. She rubbed subconsciously at the marks on her arm, and headed for the door.

It opened as she reached it.

Candy drew back in surprise. A man stood waiting, his hands hidden in the pockets of a dark trenchcoat. A wide-brimmed black hat cast tenebrous shadows over his face.

"You've got the wrong room, mister," said Candy, as she tried to compose herself.

"I don't think so," said the man in a low growl.

"Oh, I'd know. I just finished. Have you spoken to Mar—"

"She told me to come straight up."

Candy hesitated. Did she believe him? Yeah, probably. Martha treated the girls like a factory conveyer belt, especially on busy nights. She didn't like too many men waiting in the reception area. Being around other males seemed to make them nervous, even scare them off.

"I've got money," he said. "Lots of money."

"And she told you to come to me?"

"She told me to come to room twelve. This *is* room twelve?"

Candy tried to smile. She flicked her eyes to the big metal twelve crookedly affixed to the door. "That's what it says."

"Then may I come in?"

She had the sudden absurd idea that he was a vampire and needed to be invited in.

*Don't be stupid!*

"Of course. I'm sorry. Make yourself comfortable. I'm gonna head downstairs and freshen up. I won't be a minute."

She stepped aside to let him enter. He remained motionless in the doorway.

"You don't need to do that. I want you as you are."

"Look mister, that's fine, but—"

He removed a leather-gloved hand from his pocket. In it, he clutched a wad of notes half-an-inch thick. Candy swallowed a gasp, though she could do nothing to hide her widening eyes.

"I told you, I have money," said the man. "And I intend to spend it."

She had never *seen* so much money. Her heart quickened at the thought of it, though trepidation offset her excitement. In her experience, the richest guys were the kinkiest. They didn't come here to escape from loneliness. They came looking for kicks. They came to humiliate and bully, to wallow in the sordid depths of human experience. Still... she needed the money. A few ten dollar tips could only go so far. They might pay last month's rent, but not this month's. And they wouldn't put food on the table. She thought about the cupboards in the rented apartment she shared with three other girls, cupboards that were bare apart from packets of noodles and the occasional cockroach.

*So he might be a creep. But shouldn't you at least hear him out? See what he's into?*

She smiled coyly. It was time to turn on the charm.

"Okay. I'm sorry I kept you waiting. Please, come on in."

Still he would not move.

"Switch the lights off."

"But baby, I want to see you," she purred.

He picked up a black leather bag from the floor and unzipped it. Candy tensed. It was unusual for johns to bring any... extras. She relaxed as he pulled two chunky candles from the bag and held them out to her in his gloved hand.

"Light these."

She took them from him. They were surprisingly heavy.

"Oh, I like it," she said, trying to put him at ease. "Candlelight turns me on." She sashayed across the floor, and placed the candles on either side of the bed, bending over, aware that her skirt would ride up and give him a peek at her ass.

She lit the first candle with her lighter, and the overhead bulb went out.

"You like the darkness, baby?" she said. A floorboard behind her creaked. He had stepped inside. The door closed gently.

She turned to look at him. The candlelight danced across his coat, reflecting on the slick surface, his face still shrouded in darkness.

"The other candle," he said.

"Sure thing." She crawled over the bed and lit the second one, then lay back against the pillow, stretching languorously. "I like the dark. It makes me feel sexy." He stood there, saying nothing. She put a finger to her mouth and licked the tip, tracing it around her lips. "Do *you* think I'm sexy?"

No reply.

Candy sighed. "Look, mister. Can we speed this along? I don't have all night."

She reached for the fastener on her skirt.

"Don't," he said, taking a step towards her.

*At fucking last,* she thought.

She gazed up at him. "Tell me what you want, sugar. Martha probably told you about our rates. Twenty-five for standard, fifty for the full experience." She saw him nod, and continued. "But I have my *own* rates. For special customers like you." She got onto her knees and crawled towards him across the bed, the springs in the old mattress groaning beneath her. "For one hundred dollars, I'll show you the time of your life. I'll give you an experience you'll *never* forget."

"I want to tie you up," he said. For a fleeting moment, she thought she recognized his voice.

"Well..." she said. She didn't know this man. He could be anyone. A pervert, or a sicko. She wasn't averse to being tied up. Under the right circumstances, she enjoyed it. But she rarely let clients do it, and even then, only if she trusted them. It left her too helpless. "I don't usually do that. Not with new clients."

"I have money."

She scratched at her neck. "Yeah, I know. But..."

"How much?"

"Look, I told you. We can do anything else. I have *no* inhibitions. But I'm not letting you tie me up. I'm sorry."

He reached deep into his other pocket and produced another handful of bills. He tossed them onto the bed.

"Jesus Christ," she breathed. There had to be thousands of dollars there. That wasn't just last month's rent. That was the rest of the *year,* and the end of financial trouble, at least until she graduated. She took the bills in her hand, leafing through them. They were legit. With this, she could eat proper food, not survive on bagels and slices of cold pizza she found in the trash. She could send her mom a postcard without having to worry about whether she could afford the stamp. Hell, she could *call* her mom, or buy that dress she had her eye on, or invest some of it, save it for opening her boutique.

The man leaned over and pulled a coil of weathered

rope from his bag. It dangled from his hand like a used condom.

*Don't do it. Who is this guy?*

Did it matter? What's the worst that could happen?

*He could kill you.*

But not in here. Not in a brothel. That was one of the reasons she chose to work here rather than on the streets. It was safer. There were people around. There were witnesses.

She looked up at the man's face, the light from the candles revealing a black scarf wrapped around it. She had a few clients who came in disguise. Usually the wealthier ones. Politicians, actors, sports stars... while some of her johns were only able to have sex by paying for it, others used money to buy something *other* than sex — discretion. They could indulge their darkest desires without fear of it being splashed across the headlines of the *National Enquirer*.

"What are you gonna do to me?" asked Candy.

"What do you think?"

"That's not an answer."

The man waited, then spoke. "I'm going to make love to you."

*Make love?* She almost laughed, relaxing a little. Okay, this guy was most certainly *not* a killer. A weirdo, perhaps. Or an everyday, garden-variety loony. But not a *murderer*.

She took a last look at the money, then held her hands out, wrists together.

"Okay," she said. "Tie me up. But don't come in my hair or on my face, okay? Tits will be fine."

The man took the rope and reverentially wrapped it around her wrists. He tied it in a tight knot, then led her away from the bed towards the wall. Candy followed. She wasn't sure if he wanted her to struggle or not. Was this some kind of rape fantasy? Well, as long as it didn't get violent, that was fine.

A metal pipe ran overhead, and the man threw the end of the rope over it. He pulled it taut, almost lifting Candy off her feet.

"Hey, that's too high!" She stretched until her toes scraped the wooden floor, feeling herself swing. "Let me down a little, okay, honey?"

He lowered her until her soles rested on the floor. It was a promising development. He attached the rope to the door handle, tying it once, twice, then a third time.

"Hey, come on," said Candy. "That's overkill, don't you think?"

She glanced up at the pipe, wondering if she would be able to free herself should the need arise. Was she being paranoid? Yes. But in her line of work, it often paid to be.

The man locked the door with the latch and walked towards her.

"We can begin," he said.

It was only then she realized she should have taken the money upfront. What if he left her hanging here and walked away without paying? Christ, she hadn't been thinking straight. The money had dazzled her. So much of it. A life changing amount.

The man removed one glove and let it drop to the floor.

"This really turns me on," lied Candy, her voice tremulous. She realized she was afraid.

The man discarded the other glove, then opened the leather bag.

"What you got there, honey?" she asked, and she could hear it in her voice now, *really* hear it. The fear. It gripped her in a chokehold, her insides churning like her ribcage was shrinking.

The man pulled something from the bag. It glistened in the candlelight.

"What is that?"

He came towards her. Slowly, so slowly.

She saw the knife in his hands.

*Oh god, his hands...*

She knew those hands. Those awful, terrible hands, with ragged nails that earlier that evening had clamped down on her arm and cut her open.

"No," said Candy, as he removed his hat and scarf, exposing the vacant, skinless face of the priest.

*"God will judge the adulterer, and all the sexually immoral,"* he said. He raised the knife, staring at it, his mouth curling. "Hebrews, 13:4."

He put his hand to her head and cradled it, his fingers sinking into her hair.

"Are you ready to be judged?"

**5**

---

A million thoughts raced through Candy's mind at once.

She tried to latch onto one, to make sense of it, but as the priest pressed the tip of the knife to her stomach, she went utterly, hopelessly blank.

"Please," she said, as the blade jabbed through the metal mesh of her top, its cold hardness piercing her skin. She breathed in, trying to put distance between the blade and her soft, soft flesh. "Whatever you're doing, just stop."

"Whore," he said, and spat on the floor.

"Let me down," said Candy. "Or I'll scream. In ten seconds, there'll be a whole lotta people kicking that door down."

"Let them come. Let them be judged. Let *all* the sinners be judged. You are but the first of many."

He raised the knife to her face. She tried to turn, but he gripped her hair.

"All shall stand before the Lord."

The knife pressed against her cheek. Not hard enough to draw blood, but enough to let her know it was there.

Should she scream? Could anyone even hear her up here on the second floor? Music played from all around, different songs from different radios competing with one another, while upstairs was empty, the third and fourth floors abandoned and unfurnished. And if someone *did* hear her, what then? How long until they arrived and kicked down the door? What if the priest panicked and killed her?

He traced the knife down her face and neck until it rested on her collarbone. She shuddered at the sensation. The thin strap of her top gave way with one quick wrist motion, the garment sagging to her waist and sliding down her body. The priest looked at her breasts with a gaze that brought a strange sense of familiarity to Candy. He might be a killer, she thought, but he still lusted after her. It was right there in his eyes.

She used the idea to center herself, needing to find an advantage.

"I'll do whatever you want," she said, licking her lips and attempting to smile demurely. *"Anything.* Just don't hurt me."

She could kick him. She could slam her knee between his legs like she had back in the alley, maybe burst his balls open like rotten tomatoes. But what good would that do? He would take a few seconds to recover, then gut her. She was bound and helpless, and her only chance was to talk her way out of it.

A sharp pain in her left breast.

Candy flinched as the blade scratched at her nipple.

"You are guilty in the eyes of God," said the priest. "Guilty of fornication, of spiritual decay, and of immorality."

"It's just a job. It's just *sex.*"

He gently twisted the knife into her breast. Candy's body shook. She wanted to cry, but the adrenaline wouldn't let her. She looked down, wide eyed and terrified, at the blade, and at the small trickle of blood that ran down the curve of her breast.

*"Fornicator."*

The priest withdrew the knife, sliding it soundlessly out of her body. Her knees weakened and her posture slumped, increasing the pressure of the bindings on her wrists. Dust mites drifted down from above, swirling through the dim candlelight. She looked up and saw that part of the ceiling, where the pipe was affixed, had started to buckle under her weight.

The priest's revolting, clawed hand reached for her skirt, fumbling clumsily with the fastener. Giving up, he hacked at the material with the knife. As he did so, Candy pulled down hard. The pipe groaned, but moved no further. She tried lifting her feet off the ground as the priest stripped her of her leather skirt. The fabric smacked against the floor, and she stood before him in nothing but her panties, a ten-dollar bill protruding from the waistband. She looked him in the eyes. For someone so opposed to female sexuality, he *really* wanted to see her naked.

As if reading her mind, the priest spoke. "The vile forni-cator must stand exposed before her maker," he said. "She may beg, naked and humiliated, for forgiveness. It is up to the Lord to grant it or not. I am but a messenger, a holy vessel."

She tugged on the rope again. More plaster and dust drifted from the ceiling like a shaken snow globe. But not enough! She had to keep him talking, delay the inevitable. "So, uh, you're not gonna kill me?"

"The Lord speaks through me. My eyes are His eyes, my hands are His hands."

He tucked the blade into the waistband of her panties, the cool metal brushing through her pubic hair.

She was running out of time.

"Please," she said. "Let's talk about this."

The priest jerked his hand, snapping the elastic of her underwear, then got down on one knee like he was about to propose. He tore the shredded remains of her panties away and slapped the insides of her thighs.

"Open your legs. Let me gaze upon your sinful folds."

She complied. What else could she do? She was his prisoner. One false move, and he would—

He raised the knife, pointing it towards her vagina.

"Don't," she said, pulling harder on the rope. The pipe juddered, the ceiling threatening to give way.

The sharp edge of the blade grazed her thigh. He wouldn't... he couldn't...

"Okay, you win," she blurted out. "I repent. I repent! You hear me? *I fucking repent!*"

"My dear child," said the priest. He looked up at her with something resembling pity. "It's too late."

Candy squirmed as the knife entered her. As her stomach violently somersaulted, vomit clawed its way up her throat.

*Fuck it.*

She pushed away, the knife sliding out of her, and kicked her bare foot up. It struck the priest's hand, the weapon hurtling from his grasp and clattering across the floor. He turned to her, shocked, and she lifted herself up like a gymnast and thrust both feet into his chest with strength borne of blind, crazed panic. The connection was devastating. The priest's head whipped forward as his legs stumbled backwards. At the same moment, the pipe wrenched free from the ceiling, taking a sizeable chunk of plaster with it. The heavy load crashed down next to Candy as she landed with a thud on her spine. It jarred her, but she didn't have time to care. She was on her feet instantly.

The priest rose. He scrambled towards the knife.

"Help me!" screamed Candy. "He's trying to kill me!" The words left her throat raw. Someone *had* to hear her.

She ran at the priest. There were no other options. In the time it took to unlock the door, he would be coming for her. She had to stop him first. But more than that...

She wanted to hurt him.

For what he had done to her, she wanted to hurt him very badly indeed.

The priest reached the knife and jabbed it towards her belly. But he was old and slow, and she was fired up on adrenaline and fury. She dodged his thrust, darting to the side, and swung her bound arms over his head. The rope followed, wrapping around his neck and catching beneath his chin. She jerked her arms, trying to knock him off-balance. The rope tightened around the priest's jugular, but still he came for her, the knife held high, the blade dripping a faltering scarlet trail.

She scurried backwards, tripping over the corner of the bed and falling. The priest loomed over her, and she kicked out at him. He caught her foot with his free hand and tugged her towards him. She lay on her back, spread-eagled and watching in horror as the knife whistled through the air, aimed between her legs. She released the rope and kicked herself backwards, the blade embedding itself in the wood in front of her crotch.

The priest glared at her. She grabbed the rope again, pulling hard, forcing him onto his knees. Her fingers, numb with crazed vengeance, tightened around it, choking him. The priest's bloodshot eyes rolled into his skull, his tongue jabbing out the side of his mouth. The rope grew taut, and she held him at bay with her legs, pressing the soles of her feet against his face and armpit.

He gurgled something unintelligible.

"Help!" roared Candy. "Help me! *Help!*"

She heard footsteps pounding in the hallway, and chanced a glance at the door. There was movement out of the corner of her eye.

The priest.

He had the knife again.

It hovered in midair, and then he brought it swiftly down, slicing through the rope.

A knock at the door.

*"You all right in there?"*

"No!" shrieked Candy. Wasn't it fucking obvious? She heard the handle rattle.

*"The door's locked,"* said her would-be rescuer.

"Fucking knock it down!"

The priest crawled forwards. Candy scrambled back until she hit the wall. A force pounded against the door.

It didn't open.

"God has found you guilty," sneered the priest as he came towards her on all fours, the knife clicking metallically off the floor as he advanced. "And by God's hand *you shall die!*"

He gripped the weapon in both hands as, behind him, the door crashed open and a naked man burst in, tripping over his own feet and landing on the bed.

The priest turned to look, and Candy pushed off from the wall, throwing herself at him. Her bound hands found the knife, grappling it from his fingers, twisting the handle until the blade pointed towards his torso.

With all her strength, she stabbed it into his gut.

Blood sprayed from the priest's belly, as Candy tore the

knife free and brought it down again, aiming for the priest's heart, *finding* it. As she wrenched the blade out, a geyser of blood erupted from his chest, spraying across the walls.

He thrashed beneath her in a deranged tangle of limbs, knocking the weapon from her hands. Candy raised her clenched fists above her head and brought them down on his face. The man's nose shattered, the soft organ turning to mulch. *Again,* this time his front teeth tearing through the gums until they pointed inwards towards his throat. *Again,* his cheekbone cracking, his face a bloody red mess. *Again, and again, and again,* until the grotesque visage was barely recognizable as human, and then suddenly Linda was by her side, hugging her, telling her it was over and that everything was going to be okay.

Candy's arms drooped to her sides, and she let Linda hold her, though she wasn't listening.

The naked man on the bed — the one who had broken down the door and saved her life — stared at them both. He glanced at the mutilated body of the priest, his large erection wilting as fast as an ice cream melting on a hot summer's day.

The sight of it made Candy laugh. She couldn't stop. The laughter was so bizarre and alien to her ears that she wondered if she had lost her mind.

The naked man got to his feet, turning his attention to the mess on the floor.

"Shit, is he dead?"

Linda shared a glance with Candy, then looked at the priest, a pool of blood widening around the mashed pulp of his head.

"Yeah," Linda said quietly. "I'd say he's pretty fucking dead."

## 6

Candy wept against Linda's shoulder as the girl tenderly stroked her hair. The stench of blood filled the air, cloying and sickly sweet.

"Fuck me sideways," said the naked man. Candy recognized him as one of Linda's regulars. Vern. A nice guy, according to Linda. He rubbed at his eyes in cartoonish astonishment. "Man, you really did a number on him. Ho-lee *shit.*"

"He was trying to..." started Candy. "He was trying to—"

"Shhh," said Linda, her breath warm on Candy's ear. "It's okay. Everything's gonna be fine."

"The fuck it is," said the man. He sounded impressed. "That guy's all over the walls. Shit, some of him's on the *ceiling.*"

"Shut up, Vern," said Linda. "You're not helping."

"Hey, I only came here for some light relief." He gazed in awe at the pitiful sight of the priest. "Fuck. And I thought *I'd* had a bad day."

"Vern, go wait outside."

"Sure thing." He hesitated. "Listen, darling... if the, uh, cops come sniffing around..."

"I never saw you in my life," said Linda.

"Groovy." He ran a hand through his hair, which stuck up at the back from where his head had been squashed against the pillow. "And about tonight. Ya know, we never finished..."

"Next time is on the house."

That made him smile. "Groovy," he repeated. "I'm gonna get my clothes." He turned to leave.

"Wait," said Candy. She raised her head from Linda's bony shoulder and tried to smile at Vern. "Thank you. He was... he was going to kill me."

"Hey, no problemo." He took one last look at the corpse, and shook his head in disbelief... or was it admiration? "Jesus, that's gonna be a *bitch* to clean up."

With that, Vern left the room. Candy listened to his footsteps receding down the hallway, until they were obscured by KISS's *Shandi* playing from a nearby radio.

"What the hell happened?" asked Linda, casting a brief glance at the bloody figure. "Who was he?"

"The priest," whispered Candy.

"Father Patrick? Shit, that figures."

"I couldn't see his face. I recognized his voice, but I couldn't place it. I'm so stupid."

"Hey," said Linda forcefully. She turned Candy's face towards hers. "Don't even *think* about blaming yourself. This was not your fault, right?"

Candy nodded. She felt sick, and couldn't stop crying, even though she surely had no tears left. His blood felt unclean on her skin, and this final grotesque invasion of her body repulsed her.

"I need to wash this off," she said. Her throat was tight, and breathing no longer came easily.

Linda held onto her shoulders. "You do that. I'll get Martha." She glanced one more time at the dead body. "She'll know what to do."

With Linda's help, Candy staggered towards the en suite washroom where she had cleaned herself only moments before. There was no basin; just a broken mirror, a bucket, and a hole in the corner that carried the water through the building, depositing it in the river outside.

A sponge floated in the bucket. It was well used, but right now, Candy didn't care. She picked it up and stared at herself in the remaining fragments of the mirror.

A nightmare.

That's what she looked like. A grisly, terrible nightmare.

She scrubbed at her face until she could see it again. She scrubbed at her arms, her chest, her belly, trying to remove every last speck of the priest's blood. She scrubbed hard, too hard, leaving red, raw marks on her skin. For some reason, she kept thinking about her mom, and how she wanted to curl up beside her on the sofa and watch some dumb movie. Her breast hurt, and she dabbed at the cut above her nipple.

She had come close to dying tonight. About as close as it was possible to get.

"But you didn't," she mumbled to her reflection.

Watery red fluid trickled down her legs and swirled around the drainage pipe, yet no matter how hard she tried, she couldn't seem to remove the matted blood from her hair.

*Killer.*

She closed her eyes.

*You killed a man.*

She tried to think of something, anything else. Why had

she agreed to it? Why had she chosen to put herself in such a dangerous—

The money.

"Shit," she breathed.

All that fucking money... where was it? Would it still be on the bed? She had to get to it, had to find and hide it before—

She shoved open the door, and there, kneeling by the corpse, was Martha. Linda stood behind her in a short transparent dress, chewing on a fingernail. They both looked at her.

"What the *fuck* did you do?" asked Martha. She sounded mildly annoyed, like a disapproving parent.

Candy's eyes betrayed her. They shot to the bed, to the two thick wads of bills held together by rubber bands. Martha was on her feet instantly. The old bitch could *smell* money.

"That's mine," said Candy. Her voice was weak, her throat ragged from screaming.

Martha picked up the bills and inspected them. "I don't see your name on them."

"He paid me to—"

"To what? To fucking kill him? On *my* premises? If you're lucky, this *might* cover the damages."

All Candy could do was hold back more tears. This was not the time for an argument with her boss.

"What are you gonna do?" Linda asked the older woman.

Martha was too busy counting the money to look at her. "The question," she said distractedly, "is not what am *I* going to do. It's what are *we* going to do?" She glared at Candy. "After all, this is *your* fucking mess."

"I want to go home," said Candy.

"You're not going anywhere," said Martha. "None of us are. Not until this is dealt with." She looked at the corpse. "Who is it?"

"The priest," answered Linda. "Father Patrick. He tried to kill Candy." She smiled reassuringly at her. "It was self defense, right?"

"Yeah."

Martha snorted. "That's not how the cops will see it. They've been sniffing around for months now, looking for a reason to shut me down. And you've gone and handed it to them on a silver fucking plate."

"So what do we do?" asked Linda.

"What do you think? We get rid of him."

"We can't do that," said Candy.

Martha spun on her heels and faced her. "You got a better idea?" She advanced, forcing Candy to take a step back. "You just murdered a *priest*, little girl."

"He was going to—"

"You smashed his face so badly his own *mother* wouldn't recognize him."

"He was—"

Martha struck her across the cheek. "I *know* what he was going to do. But don't you understand? It doesn't *matter*. Not to the cops. Not to the press. Not to anyone. A hooker kills a priest, and thousands of dollars go missing? Who do you think is going to take the blame?"

She was right. It hurt Candy to admit it, but she was right.

"Any other witnesses?" asked Martha. She paced across the floor, peering out the door and down the corridor.

"No," said Linda. "Well, Vern, but he—"

"Who?"

"Vern. My client. He won't say anything."

"Where is he now?"

"I don't know. He went to get dressed."

Martha inhaled deeply. "Well, *find* him." She removed the stash from her pocket, counted out one hundred dollars, and handed it to Linda. "Give him this, then fuck his brains out, and make *sure* he doesn't talk."

Linda nodded and made for the door. Martha stopped her. "And send another girl up. One of the more trustworthy ones."

"Okay," said Linda.

"And get some clothes for *her*," said Martha, gesturing towards Candy.

"Sure," said Linda.

Martha grabbed her shoulder. "And hurry up about it."

"I'm *trying*." She shook free and started down the hallway.

Candy stood shivering. The air con blasted against her wet, naked skin. She watched Martha as the woman scratched at her chin, deep in thought. Her own clothes lay torn on the floor, soaked in blood.

"Strip the bed," said Martha.

"Huh?"

"Strip the bed. We can use the sheet to carry him."

The thought of staying in this room even a second longer disgusted her. She didn't care about her lack of clothes; she would leave right now and walk to her apartment stark naked if she had to. Anything to get away.

"I need to go home."

"The hell you do. You're not leaving until this mess is cleaned up. It's not just my business on the line, girl. It's your *life*. You wanna go to jail? You'll be doing what you do here, but you won't be getting paid for it, I'll tell you that much. Now, strip the bed, and be quick about it. This smell ain't gonna get any better."

There was no point in disagreeing. Martha was right again. She had killed a man, and it was only fair she stayed to help. Wasn't it? She couldn't think straight. Aware of Martha's penetrating gaze, she shuffled towards the bed and peeled off the stained sheets. She heard footsteps and stopped, staring at the door, waiting for the cops to burst in and cart her bare ass away in handcuffs.

A girl Candy knew as Sandra poked her head around the doorframe. She was pretty, with short black hair and more tattoos than Candy had ever seen on a person, except for Yakuza gang members in the Sonny Chiba movies she sometimes caught down at the Deuce.

"Linda said you wanted to see me?" she said nervously. Martha had a way of making *all* the girls nervous. Being sent to see Martha was like being sent to the principal's office.

"Get in and close the door. Did you bring clothes for Candy?"

Sandra nodded. "Yeah. Linda said..." She wrinkled her nose and turned towards the corner of the room. "What *is* that smell?"

She spotted the corpse. Clearly, Linda hadn't warned her. A reedy burp escaped Sandra's lips, and she gagged, shooting a hand to her mouth.

"My god," she said. "He's dead."

"Oh, really?" said Martha. "I hadn't noticed. Now give Candy the clothes."

"But he's—"

"*Now.*"

Sandra tossed the bag towards Candy. It landed at her feet.

Candy opened it and pulled out the contents like a carrion bird tearing the guts from a carcass. To her dismay, she realized the clothes belonged to Linda. She could tell by their size. Ridiculously small blue satin shorts, a red vest top, and a pair of clean panties, none of which would ever fit her curvy body.

"Put them on," snapped Martha. "We've got work to do, and I'm sick of looking at your fat ass."

"What happened?" asked Sandra, as Candy struggled to squeeze into the satin shorts, yanking them up over her thighs an inch at a time.

"Candy killed the priest," replied Martha by way of explanation.

"Shit," said Sandra, her face ghostly pale. "So what do you need me for?"

"You two are going to dispose of the body."

Sandra did not look pleased at the prospect, and Candy couldn't blame her. Oh, how she wished Foxy was here instead! She had never gotten on with Sandra. The girl was aloof. Cocky, even, like she was better than the other girls, with her punk clothes and surly attitude.

"Why me?" asked Sandra.

"Because you were in the wrong place at the wrong time," said Martha. "Now, shut up and listen. Both of you. If word of this gets out, we're done for. All of us. We need to remove any evidence that this fuck was ever here. I'll clear up the blood, and you two can deal with the body. Get rid of it, permanently, and I'll give you two hundred dollars each."

Sandra's eyes lit up. "Two hundred?"

Martha smiled. "That's right. For additional services." She paused. "And for your silence, naturally."

They both turned to Candy, awaiting her response. She stood before them, fidgeting in her tiny vest and shorts that all but disappeared between her ample ass cheeks. She took a deep breath and looked Martha dead in the eyes.

"Five hundred," she said. *"Each."*

Martha regarded her coolly. "Pardon? I must be going deaf. I'm trying to help you dispose of the priest you murdered, and you're *negotiating* with me?"

Candy stood her ground. This was Martha's problem too, and they both knew it. "Five hundred, no less. I know how much money he had."

"What's she talking about?" asked Sandra.

Martha waved a dismissive hand. "Fine," she said quickly, eager to move on. *"Three* hundred each. And not a cent more, or I'll make sure you can't sell your asses within one hundred miles of New York, understand?"

"Yeah, I understand," said Candy.

"Whatever," said Sandra. "For three hundred bucks, I'll eat that dead guy's ass."

"I doubt that'll be necessary," said Martha. She stood by the door and glanced furtively down the corridor. "Come on. Let's get this over with."

# 7

THEY LAID THE BED SHEET OUT ALONGSIDE THE CORPSE LIKE A crumpled white body bag, and stood at either end. As the blood soaked through the cheap polyester fabric, Candy put a hand to her mouth and looked away.

"You'll get used to it," said Sandra. "Just think of it as… roadkill."

"That was a *man.*"

"It doesn't have to be. Not anymore."

Candy closed her eyes. How could Sandra be so cold? After the initial shock of seeing the body, the young punk had acted like nothing fazed her.

Sandra kneeled by the priest's feet and looked up at her. "Want to swap ends?"

"No. It's… it's fine."

It wasn't, and they both knew it. Sandra offered her an uncharacteristically warm smile.

"Think of the three hundred bucks."

*It could have been a lot more,* Candy nearly said.

Martha entered the room carrying a mop and bucket, the soapy water spilling over the sides.

"Fuck me, enjoying the view?" she snarled. "Get rid of him before someone sees."

Candy looked at Sandra, both girls waiting for the other to make the first move.

"Come on, you got this," said Sandra. "I'll be with you every step of the way."

It was easy for *her* to say. Sandra was nothing more than a bystander. She hadn't killed a man. She hadn't almost died.

Steeling herself, Candy crouched. The satin fabric of Linda's shorts wedged painfully up her ass, and she wriggled in discomfort.

"Guess no one's gonna fit into Linda's shorts," said Sandra. She glanced at Martha, who was busy washing blood from the floor, and smiled again. "Except maybe that mop." The smile seemed genuine. "Hey, I'm sure I've got something in your size."

The offer surprised Candy. Was Sandra trying to trick her, or make fun of her? If so, this was hardly the time to do it.

"It's okay," she said. "My other clothes are downstairs."

"You're not wearing those corduroy pants while you're working under *my* roof," said Martha. "Now get the fuck out of here, both of you. And Sandra — once you're finished, give Candy some slutty clothes to wear. You're meant to be hookers, not housewives."

Sandra ignored her and held the priest's ankles, while Candy placed her hands on the dead man's shoulders. Together, they rolled him onto the sheet. His heavy body splatted face-first onto the fabric. The sound turned Candy's stomach. Part of his head remained on the wooden floorboards, a thick soup of blood and bone fragments.

Candy's head swam, and she put her hand on the floor

to maintain her balance. At least face down, the worst of him was hidden.

The stab wounds.

The crushed, flattened face.

She took two corners of the sheet, and Sandra grabbed the opposite ends.

"Ready?"

"Ready," said Candy through gritted teeth.

They stood, lifting the corners. The priest's body slumped into the middle of the sheet. Blood seeped through the material, but there was nothing they could do about that. Martha would have to mop up the stray droplets later.

"Take him…" started Martha, before reconsidering her wording. "Take it down to the furnace. Burn it. Burn everything. The sheets, the bag… Jesus, what's wrong now?"

The sheet had slipped through Candy's fingers, the body flopping to the floor.

*The furnace. Oh no. Oh god, please no, not there.*

"Candy? You okay?" asked Sandra.

Her body felt numb. "Not the furnace. I can't, I just—"

"You can, and you will," said Martha. "If you want to keep this job, anyway. There are plenty of girls out there waiting to take your place. Pretty girls with great tits who don't stab their johns to death like a fucking praying mantis."

"But the furnace…" said Candy.

"What about the fucking furnace?"

But she couldn't say. They would think she was crazy. She had never told *anyone* about that time in the basement…

"Nothing," she said.

"Come on," said Sandra. "Let's go. I'll be with you all the way, remember?"

Candy bent and gripped the sheet, and they started towards the door, the corpse swaying between them like a soft pendulum. Martha leaned on her mop handle and watched them leave.

"I don't wanna see either of you again until there's no trace of that... thing."

"And our money?" asked Sandra.

"You'll get your goddam money," said Martha, as she resumed sloshing the mop across the bloodstained floor. "Don't worry about that."

It was early enough in the evening for the building to still be quiet. Candy and Sandra took a right as they left the room, heading towards the back stairs, the ones that led down to the rear entrance. The corridor was carpeted with frayed rugs, and electric sconces fitted with candle-shaped bulbs and red glass shades lit the way. It had been Martha's attempt to create atmosphere, years before she realized that men weren't interested in atmosphere, not when there were naked girls willing to fuck for money.

One of the sconces flickered as they passed, buzzing lightly. Linda's energetic moans followed them from the other end of the hallway. It sounded like she was showing Vern one hell of a good time. Candy wondered how she could do it after staring at a bloodied, slaughtered corpse. Linda was a professional, all right. After this... *disposal,* Candy wanted to go straight home to bed, if Martha would let her.

The second sconce they passed also flickered. It dimmed, came back on even brighter, then the filament popped and the light went out. The girls looked at each other.

"A coincidence," said Sandra. "That's all."

"Sure. A coincidence." The reply was unconvincing to both girls' ears.

The body got heavier with each step. The sheet started to slip through Candy's fingers, so she bunched it up in her fist.

"You alright?" asked Sandra.

"Sure." What else could she say? She was anything *but* okay.

"You know if you ever need to talk..." started Sandra, her words tailing off. "Look, I know I've got a reputation. Some of the girls don't like me. *You* probably don't like me."

"It's not that, it's—"

"It's okay. I get it. I'm shy, and sometimes I come off as an asshole."

*"You're* shy?" asked Candy. She found it difficult to believe. Punk rock Sandra, who was constantly in-demand among the brothel's clientele for her talent as a dominatrix. She could reduce most men to tears within minutes, a highly prized skill some were willing to pay top dollar for.

"Yeah. I find it hard to talk to people. Especially you girls. You're all so beautiful. It's... it's intimidating."

"You're *gorgeous*. You know that, right?"

The third sconce jittered on and off again. Sandra glanced at it, then down at the sheet. "I don't think I am. But it doesn't matter. I keep to myself. I'm saving up, you know. To move to Europe. There's this place called Montmartre in Paris, where all the artists live in communes. It's really hip."

"You draw?"

"I paint."

"Oh yeah? Like, landscapes?"

Refusing to make eye contact, Sandra gazed down at the sheet. "Portraits. Mostly nudes." She swallowed. In the silence of the corridor, it was comically loud, like a bad sound effect in a film. "I'd like to paint you sometime."

"Me?"

"Yeah. You're... y'know..." she shrugged as best she could while carrying a corpse. "You're really... pretty."

"No one's ever painted me before," said Candy. "I'd like that."

Sandra looked up at her with a quizzical expression, as if searching for signs of sarcasm. "You would?"

"Sure. As long as you make me look good."

"Far out," said Sandra, and though her face was in darkness, Candy could tell she was grinning, as if both girls had momentarily forgotten they were carrying a cadaver.

They reached the door at the end of the corridor. Candy checked over her shoulder. They had left a trail of blood all the way from the room.

*Martha can deal with that too,* she thought.

Sandra pushed the unlocked door open with her butt, and they entered the dingy back stairs.

"Stinks in here," she said.

Candy agreed. No one used these stairs. They were lit only by dim emergency strip lights, and hadn't been cleaned in what looked like years, or possibly ever. The floor was thick with dust and small animal bones belonging to a bird or rodent. FIRE EXIT was printed on the wall, and someone had added a lipstick S in front of EXIT.

They began their clumsy descent, the body striking every step on the way down. They tried to lift it, but both girls were tiring. Candy noticed the cuts on her arm had opened up again.

"So how about you?" asked Sandra, as the body thumped against another step. "What's your plan?"

"My plan?"

"Well, you can't be planning on staying here forever. Don't get me wrong, as far as jobs go, it ain't too bad. But we've got a... what's that term? Oh yeah, a *limited shelf-life*, know what I mean?"

"I know," said Candy. "I'm in college. Final year of business school. Then I'm gonna open a boutique, sell my own clothes."

"You make your own clothes?"

"Well, not right now. Had to sell my sewing machine a while back. But I used to. And I've never stopped designing. Ever since I was a kid, I was sketching gowns and pants and shit like that."

"I can dig it," said Sandra. "You gotta do what you love if you wanna stay sane."

"Amen to that," said Candy. She looked down at the priest. "No offense."

There was a moment of silence.

*Too soon?*

Then Sandra giggled. Her laughter was infectious, and it made Candy giggle, too. She couldn't believe she was laughing.

"I gotta rest a second," said Sandra, as they navigated carefully around the bend and descended the stairs to the first floor. At the bottom, they lowered the body to the ground and Sandra stretched, the bones in her wrists clicking. "God, I'm so unfit. My arms are killing me."

"My fucking *ass* is killing me," said Candy.

"It takes a brave woman to wear Linda's shorts."

"You're telling me," said Candy. She turned her back on Sandra. "How does it look?"

"Like you're wearing a g-string."

Candy fidgeted, trying to pinch the fabric. "Great. If they go any further up there, I'm not sure we'll ever see them again."

"I meant what I said earlier, by the way," said Sandra. "About borrowing some clothes. I picked up my roommate's laundry on the way to work. She's about your size. You can wear one of her dresses. I'll show you after we..."

She trailed off. Candy understood. It was difficult to say out loud. What they were about to do was wrong, both morally and legally. And yet the other options were equally bad. Worse, even.

"Let's get it over with," said Candy, as she grabbed the corners of the sheet again.

Sandra pushed open the door. As this end of the corridor was rarely used, the lights were off, the darkness all-encompassing. Far away, a thin shaft of light spilled out from the waiting room, where the clients relaxed and exchanged money and small talk with Martha and the welcome girls.

"It looks quiet," said Sandra. "But it's real dark."

"We'll need a light to find the basement."

"It's the only one with a metal door," said Sandra. "We can find it."

The idea panicked Candy. "No, I really think we need a light. Like a flashlight, or a lighter or something. We can't—"

"Listen... you hear them?"

Candy listened. At first, all she heard was blood pounding in her temples. Then... voices. Men and women, laughing and flirting. There was the familiar colossal crash of the main entrance closing, then footsteps. A man stood silhouetted against the light.

*"Welcome, honey!"* said a woman, her voice echoing. *"You look like you could use a good fuck."*

Sandra was right. There were too many people around. They couldn't risk being seen, and so they would have to make their way down the corridor and into the basement in the dark.

*In the dark.*

Like last time...

"I can't do it," said Candy. Unable to keep the words in anymore, she blurted them out. The sheet slid through her tired fingers, the body thudding back to the ground.

"What's wrong? Why are you so uptight about the basement?"

Candy shook her head. Her chest constricted. "I'm sorry, I can't do it, I just can't. I *can't* go in the basement. You can't make me."

She screamed as something touched her skin.

"Hey, it's only me!" said Sandra.

Candy threw her arms around the girl in a hug. "I can't, I can't, I can't."

Sandra's hug was comforting. Strong but tender. It relaxed her a little. She recognized Sandra's perfume — Skin by Bonne Bell — as the same worn by her ex, and that helped soothe her nerves. But her thoughts kept returning to that time in the basement, that day when she had—

"You're trembling," said Sandra. "What's wrong? We've not far to go now."

Candy pulled back, her hands sliding to Sandra's waist. "It's the basement."

"What about it?" She spoke slowly, almost patronizingly, like a mother convincing her child that the boogeyman isn't real. "Candy, that's where the furnace is. It's so close, and then all this will all be over and we can get on with our lives."

"It's not that simple." Candy drew in a sharp, worried breath. It stabbed into her heart. "I saw something in there once. In the basement."

"There's a *lot* of shit in there."

That was certainly true. The basement had emerged miraculously unscathed from the fire that had reduced the old church to ashes. It was piled high with pews and crosses and boxes. Martha had never bothered to remove any of it. What would be the point? It wasn't in anyone's way down there, because no one went into the basement. Not unless they had to.

"Back when I first started," said Candy, "Martha used to keep the linens down there, before it got too damp."

"I remember," said Sandra.

"Some john had puked all over the bed — and all over Foxy — so Martha sent me to get a change of sheets. It was my first time down there. My last time, too." She paused. "You believe in ghosts, Sandra?"

"Yeah, I do."

Candy held the girl tighter, pressing against her. "I didn't. Not until that night. The light wasn't working. I had a candle with me, but there's a draft down there. The flame kept flickering, threatening to go out."

*Kinda like the lights have been doing all along the corridor,* she thought.

"I made it down the stairs okay, I guess. Took me forever, and I had to count each step out loud because my voice drowned out the noises I could hear, but... I *did* make it. I was so damn scared, though. It felt like there was someone down there with me, y'know? Those noises..." She shuddered at the recollection. "Like something was in the walls, or the floor, scratching to get through."

"It was rats, that's all."

"That's what I told myself. But rats don't whisper your name, Sandra. Rats don't call to you, not like that thing in the basement did. The candle kept flickering, the room getting darker. I thought I was gonna pee myself. I couldn't take it anymore, so I ran. To hell with Martha's sheets, y'know? I knew she'd be mad, but there was something in there with me, I swear it. And then..." She closed her eyes, unsure if she could continue her story.

"What happened?" urged Sandra.

"Then... I couldn't find the door. I swear on my life, it was gone. Everything was. The door, the steps, the furnace... everything was *gone*. And that's when I saw it."

"Saw what?"

"The church. For a few seconds, I wasn't in the basement anymore. I was in the old church. It was dark, hard to see. There were cobwebs everywhere, all over the pews and the lights, and I started to scream... and then I noticed the man. At least, I think it was a man. It was a shape, sitting near the front. He stood up. I wanted to run, but I was frozen."

She took a breath, her hands shaking.

"He walked towards me. I couldn't see who he was. *What* he was. The moonlight streamed in through the stained glass windows, and when he passed them, I caught glimpses of his face. I think he was—"

*"Jesus Christ, are you girls still down there?"*

Candy and Sandra looked up, still in each other's arms. Martha's ghostly pale face peered back at them from the first floor.

"What are you doing, kissing? Get rid of that fucking thing, *now*. You can screw each other on your own time."

The girls separated.

"Sorry," Sandra called up. She gave Candy's forearm arm a gentle squeeze, then retreated to her end of the sheet. "Right, let's do this. And hey, I won't let anything happen to you, okay?"

"Okay," said Candy, though she wasn't sure the word was audible. She picked up her corners, and together they shuffled into the corridor. The door closed behind them, and they were alone once more.

*All three of us.*

Each tentative step brought them closer to the basement door.

"God, did you hear her?" said Sandra. "She thought we were kissing. That's dumb, huh?"

"Yeah," said Candy, only half-listening.

"As if you'd be into someone like me."

She wished she hadn't told the story about the basement. There was no need to dredge up those old, ugly memories. It had been a hallucination brought on by fear, that was all. Now, what was Sandra saying?

"I bet your boyfriend would think that was funny," said Sandra.

"My what? Oh, I don't have a boyfriend."

"Maybe your girlfriend?"

Tremors rippled through Candy's body. Once again, she heard nothing but the blood pumping through her veins, and her head was beginning to throb.

"You find the door yet?" she managed to ask.

"Not yet."

Candy noticed the disappointment in the girl's voice. Had Sandra asked a question? She couldn't be sure. She heard a noise and turned. A scratching.

*It's in your head.*

She watched Sandra grip the sheet with one hand and rap her knuckles off each door they passed. Each one offered the same response; a hollow, wooden emptiness. What was even *behind* these doors? Where did they lead to?

Sandra continued gently knocking each door, listening for the tell-tale sound of the basement's metal door.

Wooden.

Wooden.

Wooden.

Candy wanted nothing more than to drop the body and call the cops. Hell, prison couldn't be worse than what was down in that infernal basement.

A light chiming sound reverberated softly through the corridor as Sandra's knuckles struck metal.

"Found it," she said.

Tears sprang to Candy's eyes. Moving on autopilot, she said nothing, her limbs carrying her onwards.

The door handle creaked.

"Is that you?" asked Candy.

"Yeah. Stay cool. You're with me, remember?"

The door groaned open on rusted, ancient hinges. Immediately, a gust of frigid air gasped free from the basement, carrying with it the stale scent of damp and rotted wood. Sandra reached in and groped for the light switch. There was a faint click, but no light.

"Bulb must have blown."

"Of course it fucking has," muttered Candy. She knew it wouldn't work. It was inevitable. It was fate.

It was her karmic comeuppance.

"I'll go first," said Sandra.

"I don't think I can do it," said Candy.

"You can. How many steps did you count last time?"

"Ten."

"Well then, let's toss this piece of shit down the stairs, and we can count them together. One step at a time, whaddya say?"

Candy's mouth was dry. She tried and failed to swallow. "Okay," she said, her lips smacking together. She followed Sandra through the door and stood at the top of the stairs. It was so dark inside she could barely see the other girl.

"We'll swing him, and let go on three. You ready?"

"Mm-hmm," said Candy. It was the best response she could muster.

"Okay, you ready? On three... one... two... *three!*"

Candy released the sheet in time with Sandra. The blood-soaked bundle flew through the air, dropping quickly. It bounded off a step halfway down, then another, and landed with a thud on the packed dirt of the basement floor. Candy squinted into the darkness. The vague white shape waited there like a ghost.

"See?" said Sandra. "It's not far, is it?"

"What if he's still down here?"

"He's dead, Candy. He's not going anywhere."

Candy clenched her jaw. "No, I mean... the man from last time. The man I saw."

Sandra took her hand. "Candy, there was no one down there. And if there was, it was probably some bum coming in out of the rain or something. But there's no one there now. And if there is? We'll fuck him up. Don't forget, I'm a goddam dominatrix. I'll have him sucking on my toes and begging for a spanking in two minutes, tops."

Candy tried to smile. She appreciated Sandra putting on a show of bravado for her, though she still couldn't understand why the girl seemed so unfazed by what they were doing.

"Thanks," she said. "And you were right, you know.

About what you said before. I *didn't* like you. I thought you had an attitude, like you thought you were better than everyone else. And I'm sorry about it. I wish I'd gotten to know you sooner."

"Hey, nothing like a bit of corpse disposal to bring people together, right? Oh, I don't mean *together* like we're a couple or anything. I just mean—"

"I know what you mean."

"Okay," said Sandra. Candy heard the relief in her voice. "Then let's do this. You ready?"

The pitch black void stretched out before them, stale air brushing their skin. Candy gazed down the rickety wooden steps. She could make out four, maybe five of them. But no more.

"Ready," she said. It was a lie.

"Okay, one at a time."

Sandra stepped forward, and Candy moved with her. Her foot found the first step. The wood felt good and solid, and she rested her weight on it, her feet settling comfortably.

"One," she said.

"There, that wasn't so hard, was it?"

"I guess not."

She looked over her shoulder at the open door leading back into the corridor. The voices from the waiting room had faded to nothing, and all she could hear was the faint whisper of wind and an occasional drip.

*Blood. It's blood.*

"Ready for the next one?" asked Sandra. "Let's do it."

They took the second step. Candy tried to picture Martha checking her watch and wondering what was taking them so long, but all she could think of was—

"Two," she said, banishing the thought.

"One quarter of the way there," said Sandra.

*One fifth,* Candy almost said, but this wasn't the time for correcting Sandra's math. The girl was doing her a favor. She was helping her conquer her fear, and it was working... wasn't it?

They took the third step. Then the fourth. It was only at the fifth step when Candy's nerves started to flutter. She glanced back at the entrance.

"I can't see the door," she said. Her stomach churned, and suddenly her bladder felt very full.

"It's not gone anywhere. Come on, let's keep going."

Sandra took another step, and Candy followed. This one creaked underfoot.

"Six."

Over halfway there. Not far to go. When she was a kid, Candy used to jump down four steps like it was nothing. Should she do that now, and get it over with?

*And what if he's there? What if he catches you?*

She gripped Sandra's hand. It was so cold down here, and she felt sick. A grim odor filled her nostrils.

*The priest. We're getting closer to him.*

Another step. Candy felt Sandra nudge her arm.

"Seven," she said, though her throat was parched, and the word came out funny. She searched in vain for a signal that she was in the basement; a flickering candle, or the stack of pews, or a shapeless, malevolent silhouette striding towards her.

Nothing.

"You got this, Candy. Let's take another one."

She didn't want to, but they did. Somehow, she managed.

"Eight."

She tried to locate the white sheet containing the priest,

but couldn't. The polyester funeral shroud had to be no more than *inches* in front of them. Or was it so stained in blood that it was now soaked a deep crimson, rendering it invisible in the darkness?

"Almost there."

Sandra took the next step. Candy hesitated, then followed.

"Nine," she said. Tears flooded her eyes, and she knew without a shadow of a doubt that if she took one more step there would be nothing there, just a vast, infinite void, an infinity of horror waiting to swallow her up, and at the center of it, at the center of this evil, impossible blackness, he would be waiting for her, like he always had been, the dark man, the horror from the church, the—

"Ow, you bitch!" she screamed, as Sandra's hand gripped the back of Candy's satin shorts and yanked the waistband up in a sharp wedgie that cut deeply between her ass cheeks. She stumbled forwards as the fabric dug in, then spun towards Sandra.

"What the fuck did you do that for? You chafed my fucking asshole!"

"I'm sorry," said Sandra. "But look... you made it. You made it down the steps."

Candy quietened. She scuffed her feet in a wide arc, feeling the comforting resistance of the dirt floor. The pounding in her heart started to subside.

"Shit," she said. "I did it. I made it."

"Sorry about your ass, but I didn't think you were going to take that last one. Figured I'd help you out."

"You could have just *pushed* me."

"I coulda," said Sandra. She hopped down the final step, landing beside Candy. "But I didn't."

Candy tugged at the smooth material between her

cheeks. Any further, and the shorts would have been gone forever. She walked forwards, and her foot hit something. She stumbled and fell.

"Candy, you okay?"

She landed on the floor, bashing her knees, then whirled around, her hands searching for what had tripped her. She scrabbled through the dirt, until she found—

Something soft.

She probed further, then recoiled in horror.

It was the priest's face. Or what was left of it.

"Candy?"

"I tripped." Her heart was racing again, beating frantically against her rib cage. Any more scares and she was certain she would drop dead of a heart attack.

It was a curious thing, though. Her eyes had started to adjust to the darkness. On the stairs, they hadn't. There, the darkness had been impenetrable, absolute. But now she was here, in the basement, it seemed more... normal? Was that the word? Well, as normal as things *could* be in a brothel basement with the dead body of a priest.

In the corner, the furnace grumbled, seeking her attention. Flames sparked and crackled behind the round metal door.

*There's your scratching sound, dumbass.*

Candy got to her feet. Sandra was already walking towards the furnace. The door was sealed with a valve, a filthy rag hanging from it. Sandra put her hands on the rag and turned the valve. The sound of grinding metal assaulted their ears, only halting when Sandra pulled on the door and it shuddered open. The flames inside danced and jerked, casting a wide illumination around the basement.

Candy took in the dubious sights. It was as she remembered. Old pews were stacked against the wall, piled three high. A metal unit stood sentinel, its doors open like it had been disemboweled, spilling endless rotting bibles and pamphlets and hymn sheets onto the ground. Metal bars and poles and planks of lumber lay haphazardly against the far wall, resting alongside discarded tools and huge crates. And there, right in the center of the nearest wall, leaned an enormous wooden crucifix. The carved Christ upon it was covered in green rot and mildew, his face frozen in an eternal howl of anguish. The wood was as black as charcoal, the features burned away and indistinct.

But what bothered her most — a detail she had forgotten since that night, but which now came back to her with shocking clarity — were the hands. They seemed to face the wrong way, gripping the edges of the cross, the crooked fingers curled around the ancient timber as if the lifeless figure was attempting to claw himself free from his holy prison.

"Let's get the priest," said Sandra over the roar of the furnace, and together, they dragged the sheet towards its final resting place, leaving a shallow impression in the dirt.

Candy shrank back from the intense heat. Why was it always so *cold* in the damn building? And why was there never any hot water in the showers? These were questions she could ponder another time. Right now, she just wanted out of here.

She glanced at the stairs, but they were tantalizingly out of reach of the light. Only the trail of blood glimmered in the inferno.

So much blood in a human body.

So much *blood*.

"Ready?" said Sandra.

"Do I have a choice?"

"Does anyone?"

Candy had no answer to that, so she bent and hooked her arms under the priest's shoulders while Sandra took him by the legs. The sheet had fallen open, revealing the brutalized, pulped face of the dead man.

*You did that.*

It was undeniable. But he would have done the same to her. Hell, he would have done *worse*.

"Fuck you," she whispered venomously.

She could tell Sandra was looking at her. Thankfully, the girl said nothing. She seemed to know when to talk and when not to, which was an admirable trait. They lifted the body, struggling to angle it through the circular hole.

In a few seconds, it would all be over.

The heat prickled Candy's skin, and she turned away, but not before she saw the priest's face enter the flames. The devastation was absolute. His skin blackened, oozing thick clods of goop that sizzled in the fire.

His leg twitched, and Candy stole a glance at Sandra.

"It's just the nerves," the girl said. "It's a reflex—"

Then his whole body jerked violently, the legs kicking. A sharp knee caught Candy in the jaw and she stumbled backwards, bright lights exploding in her vision. The dead priest was in the furnace up to his waist, but his legs were a frenzied blur of motion.

"Help me!" screamed Sandra. She clung to the priest's thighs as charred black hands clamped onto the door frame. Candy was rooted to the spot. She watched in mounting horror as the priest tried to pull himself back out.

He was still alive. My god, *he was still alive.*

Sandra stared at her in wide-eyed panic. "Candy, *please!*"

Somehow, she found the strength. She raced towards the furnace, wrapping her arms around the priest's ankles, trying to get them under control. His wild kicks caught her in the chest, but she looped her arm around the errant limbs and clenched her muscles tightly, gripping his ankles in an unbreakable, vice-like hold.

"Get him inside!" screamed Sandra.

"I'm trying to!"

She lifted and pushed, but the priest remained halfway in. His torso was on fire, the flames working their way along his arms to the hands that clung desperately onto the door frame.

*He can't be alive. He can't be.*

And yet he was pulling himself out with inhuman strength. From inside the furnace came the most appalling, ghastly howl Candy had ever heard, a piercing banshee wail of incomprehensible agony. She could take no more.

Candy released the priest's ankles and ran.

"Where are you going?" shouted Sandra.

Candy ignored her. She headed for the wall, snatching up one of the metal bars from the ground, and returned to the blazing furnace. Black smoke belched from inside, the acrid stench of burning tissue and cloth seeping into the atmosphere. The priest's hands were aflame now, droplets of melting flesh sizzling as they ran down the metal exterior.

Candy drew the bar back. She took one look at the crispy black hands, and swung with all her might. The bar demolished one hand, clanging off the metal with a devastating recoil that sent tremors snaking through her limbs.

Sandra kept pushing, edging the priest further inside.

Candy maneuvred around the kicking legs and swung again, smashing the other hand to pieces. It crumbled upon impact, a couple of fingers dropping to the floor. The bar dropped from her hands and she rejoined Sandra, wrestling with the priest's legs, forcing him in up to his knees. Still his feet kicked, his shin bones cracking repulsively against the door frame, until, eventually, he was all the way in.

Sandra slammed the door, steam rising from her burning palms as she spun the valve, and then it was closed, it was *locked,* the priest gone forever, and a devastating, awful silence reigned once more in the basement.

**8**

---

CANDY EYEBALLED THE FURNACE DOOR, WATCHING, *WAITING* for it to burst open and the flaming priest to re-emerge. She stared for a long time, so long she almost forgot Sandra was there.

"He wasn't dead," she finally said, breaking the silence.

"He had to have been. He was... he was all fucked up."

"No. We killed him. We..."

She stopped herself. What did it matter? She *knew* she had killed him. What difference did it make if she killed him a second time?

*Because you had a chance to change things. To make them right.*

Not true. She would have been arrested for murder and sent to jail, her mugshot plastered on the front pages of all the papers under the lurid headline PSYCHO HOOKER SLAUGHTERS PRIEST. It wouldn't matter what she said. No one would believe her.

"He was scum," she said decisively. "I did nothing wrong."

"That's right," said Sandra. "He deserved to die." She cleared her throat. "He, uh, *did* deserve it, right?"

Candy glanced at Sandra, then remembered the girl didn't know the full story. "Yeah," she said simply. "He was going to kill me." She didn't want to get into it. The wound was too fresh. She wondered if it would ever fully heal.

"Shitheads like that..." said Sandra. "Once they get a taste for blood, they never stop. You did the right thing. *We* did the right thing. There's one less creep roaming the streets tonight. We've done the women of New York a fucking favor."

Behind the metal door, the furnace crackled menacingly. Candy imagined the priest's bones splintering in the heat and crumbling to ash. How long did it take to completely destroy the human body? How long until all traces were vaporized? Did anyone know he was here? Perhaps his grim flock of protestors? Surely not. Those idiots outside... they waved their placards and chanted their dumb slogans, but they were essentially harmless. They were many things, but not murderers.

"So what now?" she asked.

"Now... we forget about it. We move on with our lives. And we never speak about this again. Not to anyone, ever. It's over. It's *all* over."

Sandra spoke with conviction, though her words did little to reassure Candy. She could still picture the priest's ghastly face, those cold, dead eyes boring into her, fueled by righteous hatred. She could still hear his voice, his apocalyptic proclamations and disgust at her feminine body. And she could still feel the sharp edge of the blade on her skin, tracing its way down her breast, her stomach, her...

She'd never forget it.

Not for as long as she lived.

"Let's get out of here," she said. The misshapen face of the wooden Christ leered at her from the cross. She turned away from it. "I hate this place so much."

Sandra took her hand and led the way to the old staircase. They walked together in silence through the darkness, the padding of their feet oddly quiet against the dirt floor.

"Think Martha'll make us go back to work tonight?" asked Candy, though she already knew the answer. Martha probably had a couple of johns waiting for them upstairs.

Sandra said nothing.

Was the realization of what they had done only now setting in? Candy understood people processed trauma in different ways. Sandra had been there for her in a time of need, and now it was her job to offer support.

"Tell you one thing," she said, trying to lighten the mood. "I can't wait to get out of these shorts."

Nothing.

"You said you've got your friend's laundry, right?"

Sandra remained taciturn. Candy had been sure talking about her shorts would have elicited a response. It was blatantly obvious the girl had a crush on her. She squeezed Sandra's hand.

It was cold. Cold and *hard*.

"Sandra?"

Still no reply.

A door opened somewhere, clattering noisily off the wall. Dim light flooded in from the corridor, illuminating the top two stairs and no more. A figure stood in the doorway, dark and formless.

Candy's heart skipped a beat, and she forgot about Sandra's odd behavior. She took a step backwards, retreating into the darkness. Who was up there? Martha? Or maybe the cops?

The figure waited in the doorway, motionless.

*It's him, it's the man from the church, he's come to get you, he's found you, you came back down here to the basement and—*

"Candy, you in here?" the figure called out.

It took her a second to place the voice. It shouldn't have taken that long, for it was a voice she knew. A voice she had been conversing with for the last twenty minutes. Sandra's voice. But how the hell could Sandra be at the top of the stairs?

She was right beside her...

They were holding hands...

Candy froze.

Her body trembled. She stared straight ahead, looking up the stairs at Sandra.

"Candy? Can you hear me?"

Candy's mouth opened, but emitted no sound.

From beside her came an ominous, wheezing rattle.

The grip on her hand tightened, and she knew that if she turned around now, she would surely go mad.

*"Whore..."*

The voice was inhuman.

A rasping croak.

She wanted to scream, but her throat would not allow it.

The only thing she could do was close her eyes.

*"You belong in hell,"* it said, and then something touched her shoulder and everything went dark.

# 9



Candy awoke in a brightly lit room.

The light pulsed in her vision, and when she tried to sit, a hand pushed against her, pinning her down. She was too weak to resist. Through blurry eyes, she looked into the face of her attacker.

"Stay cool," said Foxy. "Just lie down. Relax. You hit your head."

Candy lay still. She blinked, attempting to clear her vision, and found she was in the first-floor room where Martha now stored the linens. The washing machine rumbled in the corner, vibrating the table she lay on.

Foxy leaned over and put her hand on Candy's forehead. "You feeling alright? Sandra found you in the basement."

"Where is Sandra?" asked Candy. "Is she okay?"

"She's fine. I helped her carry you up the stairs. What happened? Do you remember?"

Again Candy tried to sit, and this time Foxy assisted. Her head swam a little, but it wasn't too bad. The white sheet that covered her slipped down, and she realized she was topless.

"Don't worry, that was me," said Foxy. She pointed to a crudely applied dressing on Candy's breast. "You were bleeding, so I patched you up. I would have taken your shorts off too, but I think they'll need to be surgically removed."

"They're Linda's," said Candy.

"Figures. Anyway, I'm sure if you ask Sandra, she'd help. That chick's in love with you."

Candy half-smiled and lay back down, resting her eyes as a headache raged within her. She placed one hand on her forehead, while Foxy held the other. Then, like a bolt of lightning, it all came back to her. Candy's eyes shot open.

"There was someone down there. In the basement."

"Hey, it's alright. Sandra told me all about it." She twirled a strand of Candy's hair between her fingers. "It's all over. He's *gone.*"

"No, not the priest. Someone *else*. He... he..."

"Tell me later," said Foxy. "This ain't the time. Now take it easy, there's a doctor on the way."

"A doctor?"

"Yeah, he's screwing Kelly in room seven. Sandra's gone to fetch him." Foxy leaned in closer and stroked her hand down Candy's face. "I'm sorry about what happened. I wish I'd been there for you."

Tears filled Candy's eyes, the overflow spilling down her cheeks. "He was going to kill me. I had no choice."

"That's not true," said Foxy. "You did have a choice. And you made the *right* decision. If some wacko's gonna kill you, you kill him first. No second thoughts, no regrets. You did the right thing. You did what any of us would have done." Foxy wiped away one of Candy's tears. "Hell, you did exactly what *I* would have done. I'm proud of you."

Before Candy could respond, the door opened and

Sandra entered, accompanied by an older man with graying hair and round glasses. His crisp white shirt hung open, and below the waist he wore nothing but silk shorts.

"This is highly unorthodox," he was saying to Sandra in an English accent. "I don't have my bag, my equipment. There's very little I can…" He trailed off as he spotted Candy, his eyes widening at her state of undress. "Is this her? The injured party?"

"Yeah," said Foxy. "She hit her head. Been unconscious, but just woke up."

Upon seeing Candy was awake, Sandra smiled and ran to her side. "Oh my god, you're okay! I was so worried."

"What happened?" asked Candy. "Where did you go?"

"May I interrupt this charming reunion?" asked the doctor, as he shuffled his way towards her, elbowing Sandra to the side. "I was perilously close to *climaxing* a few moments ago, before I was so rudely interrupted." He laid his hands on Candy's head and raised it from the table, sliding his fingers around her scalp. "Keep still please… any pain?"

"No, none. Sandra, I— ow!" Candy glared at the doctor.

"I found it," he said. "Just a bump. She'll live."

"Is that your medical opinion, *doctor?*" said Foxy.

He ignored her, his gaze dropping to Candy's breasts. He gestured towards the dressing. "I'd, uh, better take a look at that. Could be infected."

"That won't be necessary," said Candy, pulling the sheet up to cover herself and inadvertently revealing Linda's satin shorts.

The doctor shrugged nonchalantly. "As you wish. Only trying to be of assistance, like any good medical professional. May I go now? If you don't mind, I have company waiting upstairs, and I'm rather eager to—"

"Climax," finished Foxy. "Yeah, you mentioned that already."

The doctor flashed her a wry smile, before reverting his gaze to Candy. Or, more specifically, to her crotch. "I must say, those are charming little shorts you're almost wearing. Do you work here *every* Thursday?"

"Yeah," said Candy.

"Every Thursday. How interesting. I'll make a note of that. I'd like to see you again." He smiled. It didn't look good on him. "For *medical* reasons, of course. Just a check-up." He turned towards the door, then looked back. "You will wear those shorts again, won't you?"

Without waiting for an answer — and with a very visible, growing erection — he left the room, leaving the door wide open. Foxy closed it behind him and twisted the lock with a satisfying *click*.

"So," she said. "You gonna tell me what happened?"

Candy filled her in on the evening's events as best she could, from her initial encounter with the priest in the alleyway to his death and subsequent disposal.

"The last thing I remember," she said, turning to Sandra, "is hearing you call my name."

"You were right behind me. I swear, I could hear your footsteps on the stairs. You didn't say anything, so I thought maybe you were mad at me, or in shock."

"And I thought you were mad at *me*. I was holding your hand. I was holding..." she shivered. "...*somebody's* hand."

"You were scared, that's all," said Foxy. "And understandably so. After what you'd been through..."

"No. It wasn't my imagination. I was physically touching them, for real. And... and they spoke to me."

"What did they say?"

"Whore. They called me a whore."

Foxy smiled. "Well, they weren't wrong. But it doesn't matter, because it's all in the past now. What's done is done, and you don't ever have to go into that basement again."

A chill skittered through Candy's body at the thought. Even the idea that she was close to it, that she would have to walk by that entrance, that somebody — or some*thing* — was still down there, waiting for her, calling to her...

A sharp knock made the girls jump. Foxy shook her head and laughed it off, then unlocked the door. Martha shoved it open and entered, her face a gargoyle sneer. She gave Candy a quick once-over.

"How is she?" she asked, sounding more pissed-off than sincere.

"She's okay," said Foxy. "Best she lies down, takes the night off."

"If she can lie down, she can work. She's *paid* to lie down." Martha smiled at that, obviously proud of her quick-thinking.

"She needs to *rest,*" said Foxy.

Martha regarded her coolly. "She's got a client waiting."

"Who is it?" asked Candy.

"Joseph."

Joseph. One of her regulars. Mid-thirties, harmless. Always wore expensive suits and tipped well if she let him kiss her. She wasn't in the kissing mood right now, but dammit, she needed the money. She thought of the priest's cash, and of how close she had been to getting her hands on it.

*Fucking Martha.*

She rubbed at the back of her skull. The bump wasn't serious, but Joseph was a missionary position kinda guy, and even with an extra pillow behind her head, it was gonna be painful. She'd have to convince him to try doggy style tonight.

"Shit, tell him I'll be five minutes," she said.

"Baby, you don't have to do this," said Foxy.

But she *did* have to. Because if she didn't get straight back on the horse, so to speak, the fear would build up inside of her until she was never able to do it again. She tried to tell herself it was a one-off. She had slept with dozens of different men over the last year. Not quite a hundred, but a lot. And almost every one had been, if not respectful, then at least polite. They reminded her of something her mom used to say about spiders.

*They're more scared of you than you are of them.*

But all it took was one sicko to throw everything out of whack, to mess with her confidence. When she was a kid, some old wino had exposed himself to her. He had been lurking in the public bathrooms near the park, hiding in a stall. When she came out, he was standing there, his trench coat wide open, his...

She had never used a public bathroom again. Even though she was an adult now, and able to defend herself, the memory forever lingered.

*What if he's there, waiting, when I open the door?*

No, she couldn't have another phobia, no matter how rational. She was unwilling to let the behavior of a man steal another part of her soul. The damn priest wouldn't control her like that.

"It's okay, Foxy," she said decisively. "I got this."

"That's settled then," said Martha. "Get yourself cleaned up, and take that bandage off your tit. You're meant to be sexy. I trust you two," she said, eyeballing Candy and Sandra, "got rid of the problem?"

"It's dealt with," said Sandra.

Martha nodded. "Good. I've left the mop and bucket by the basement door. Clean up any residue, and let's never speak of this again." From down the corridor, a telephone rang. Martha turned to Foxy. "Answer it."

"Yes ma'am," grumbled Foxy. She winked at Candy. "Talk later, yeah?"

"Sure."

Candy swung her legs off the table, letting them dangle as Martha exited without another word, leaving her alone with Sandra. Linda's red vest lay next to her. Candy picked it up and fought her way into the slender garment.

"You gonna be okay?" asked Sandra, who had turned her back on Candy to allow her to dress. It was a simple, and wholly unnecessary, act of kindness, and it made Candy smile.

"Yeah, I think so. You?"

Sandra glanced to see if Candy was clothed. "I'll be alright." Her voice dropped to a whisper. "It's not the first body I've had to get rid of."

Candy didn't know what to say. She looked into the girl's sad eyes. "Shit, Sandra. You wanna talk about it?"

"Yes and no. Some other time, maybe. Put it this way; I understand what you went through tonight. I really do."

Candy nodded. "Well, how about a drink after work?" She smiled. "We can talk about that painting you're gonna do of me."

"You mean that?"

"Yeah. I'd like to." She slid off the table and leaned against it, getting accustomed to standing again. Her head still throbbed, though it was less intense than before. "Now... where's that dress you promised me?"

"In my locker," grinned Sandra, as they left the store room and headed down the corridor. "Though for what it's worth, I... I think those shorts look great on you."

Warmth spread across Candy's face. "Thanks," she said, lightly nudging Sandra with her elbow. The skin-on-skin contact felt strangely reassuring. Except for her banter with Foxy, she was always self-conscious when flirting. *Seriously* flirting, not like when she was with the men. That was an act, a game of make-believe. This was different. There was intent behind it, and Candy was in no doubt the feelings were reciprocated.

"Don't go down there," she said suddenly.

"Where?"

"The basement. Just tell Martha you cleaned it. She'll never know."

They entered through the beaded curtain and Sandra went to her locker. "I'll be okay," she said. "Don't worry about me. We've already been down there." She pulled out a heavy bag and unclasped it. "It's me and my roommate's laundry, so it's all clean, I promise."

Sandra emptied the bag. Eventually, surrounded by mounds of socks and underwear and leather pants, and a seemingly inexhaustible supply of black tees, she produced a blue cotton sundress. Hardly attire suitable for fall in New York, Candy thought, but it was better than nothing, and at least it looked like it would fit. She took it from Sandra and held it up to herself.

"Perfect," she said. "And thanks again for tonight. For *everything*. I couldn't have done it without you."

Sandra's cheeks flushed bright red. "It's okay. No problem."

Candy put her arm on the girl's waist, leaned in, and kissed her. It was quick and delicate and intoxicating, a brief glimmer of humanity amongst the horrors of the evening. Her hand slid down to Sandra's ass and playfully smacked it.

"Now get outta here," she said. "I'm gonna take a quick shower."

Sandra licked her lips. "Okay," she stammered. "Yeah. Okay. I'll... yeah."

"See you later," said Candy.

"Yeah."

"You said that already."

"Ye—" She caught herself. "Later," she smiled. Candy had never seen a face so utterly crimson. Sandra walked to the door and pushed. It wouldn't open.

"Pull," said Candy.

Sandra turned to her, still smiling her embarrassed little smile, and said, "So it is." She pulled the door open. It hit off her foot and jolted. "Damn door," she said, and hurriedly slipped through the narrow gap as if she was escaping from a burning building.

Candy stifled a laugh. The poor girl. How the hell did she manage to keep her composure with her johns? Though she knew it was different with men. It was for *her,* anyway. There was no danger of attraction, no fear of rejection.

Boisterous female voices boomed through the corridor. More girls starting their shift, or perhaps finishing for the night. The building was open sixteen hours a day, twenty four if there were enough appointments. Sex waited for no one these days.

She wanted to be in the shower before they arrived, so she hooked her thumbs into the waistband of the satin shorts and wrestled them down over her thighs. She heard a slight tear.

"Sorry, Linda."

She wondered how the girl was getting on. Was she still giving Vern his compensation? One hundred dollars and a night of free sex, not bad going for ol' Vern. She made a mental note to collect her three hundred from Martha, and to make sure Sandra got her cut, too. The thought of Sandra's red face made her smile again. The kiss, so brief yet so exquisite. It had been a while since she'd kissed someone and meant it, and she had almost forgotten how good it felt.

Oh, she knew she shouldn't mix business with pleasure, but it wasn't like she was going on a date with one of her clients. A date? Was that what it was?

"Yeah," she said. "A date."

Then the other girls burst through the door, laughing and chatting happily, blissfully unaware of what had transpired within these walls tonight, and Candy smiled and said hello to them and disappeared into the shower.

She tried not to think about the priest, or the basement.

And she especially tried not to think about whose hand she had been holding.

**10**

———

The mop was waiting for Sandra by the basement door.

It rested in a bucket of reddish water, a long trail of which led down the corridor and into the darkness. Martha had done a pretty poor job of cleaning up, though Sandra was happy to finish it for her. It was better than feigning indescribable pleasure at some jerk's clumsy touch for the next hour. Plus, there were three *hundred* dollars waiting for her.

Not to mention a date with Candy.

She smiled to herself. She knew she shouldn't be happy. How could she be, after what she had done? A man's body was burning in the furnace, and she had helped put him there. But Sandra was no stranger to death. Was it any different to how she spent her childhood, assisting her father in the funeral home? There, she had wheeled bodies through endless antiseptic corridors to their final destination — the crematorium. For the open casket ceremonies, she prepared the faces of the men and women and children. In the easiest instances — where death had been natural, whatever that meant — she simply applied makeup to create the illusion of life and vitality. Sometimes, however, she was forced to reconstruct the faces using wax and clay. Highway accidents were the worst. Gunshot victims weren't too bad, unless the weapon had been something like a shotgun, but the damage incurred from a face slamming into a steering wheel or a dashboard at seventy miles per hour was absolute. It was why Sandra *always* wore a seat belt.

Even when, tired and crying, she had driven to the desert to dispose of her father's corpse.

To the best of her knowledge, her father was still buried there, and long may he rot. After what he had done to her, the bastard deserved it. They had been so close, once upon a time. Daddy's little girl, that's what he used to call her.

It was why she assumed she could tell him about her sexual orientation. About how she thought she was a lesbian. Actually, screw it, she didn't *think*. She *knew*, and had for a long time.

She thought her father — a kind man, and a decent man, she had always believed — would understand, and not send her to a clinic where men in white coats attached electrodes to her wrists and ankles and sent shocks sparking through her body if she didn't respond quickly enough to visual stimuli.

And yet that was precisely what he did.

Sandra spent four months in that awful place, tortured daily by a group of medical sadists using a sick combination of science and religion to 'cure' her.

In an attempt to get out, she played along with their tests. They showed her images of nude men, and she had to press a button to move to the next slide. If a nude woman appeared and she didn't click the button fast enough, they would shock her. It was inhumane. One day — for reasons far from scientific — the doctors had stripped her and laughingly attached the electrodes to her breasts. As they leered at her, she slipped free of the bonds and beat them senseless, choking one man unconscious with the electrode cable and battering the other's face against the wall until he begged for mercy. But she hadn't killed them. Instead, she escaped out the window and ran for her life. She broke into a store and stole some clothes, then headed home. With no friends and no other family, she had nowhere else to go.

Arriving at the mortuary, her father greeted her at the door.

*I guess I'll just have to cure you myself,* he had said. She still remembered the pungent smell of liquor on his breath. When he started to unfasten his pants, Sandra had killed him. She hadn't meant to. She shoved him and he fell, his head hitting the corner of the hallway cabinet with a loud *pop*, dark black blood trickling down the stained wood.

Everything after that had been easy. The drive through the night with a shovel and a body in the trunk. The burial. The return home to pick up as much money and clothes as she could carry. And, finally, the cross country Greyhound bus to New York that almost wiped out her cash by the time she arrived.

And now history was repeating itself.

Sandra pushed open the door to the basement and carried the mop and bucket down the stairs, quietly hoping she would never have to dispose of a body ever again. She wondered how Candy was doing. Was that her real name? Doubtful. Most of the girls used an alias to help maintain emotional distance from the men. Sandra didn't bother. As a gay woman, keeping a distance from her johns was easy. She never let anyone get close to her, in or out of work.

A name came to her.

*Mary.*

Had she heard Foxy refer to Candy as Mary? She thought so. It was a nice name. Would Candy let her use it? Would they get that close?

"Don't get your hopes up," she said softly as she descended the stairs. Candy had kissed her, sure, but it probably meant nothing. They had experienced a shared trauma, that was all. The kiss was a thank you, a pleasant exchange between friends. Once Candy had time to think, to consider her options, she would forget about her. People *always* forgot about her.

It was what she did best. Well, that and dominating men.

As she made her way down to the basement, she realized she was counting the steps. Feeling foolish, she smiled.

"Ten," she said, as she took the last step.

It was pitch black, so she opened the furnace door. A surge of heat escaped, the flames lighting the dingy room and casting weird shadows across the walls, the wooden Christ seeming to fidget on his cross. No wonder poor Candy had been so scared.

Standing on tiptoes, she peered into the furnace. It had only been half-an-hour since they deposited the priest, but she could see no trace. Funny, that. She knew from her admittedly strange childhood that bodies took a good couple of hours to cremate. The priest had been a tall, thin man. There was less of him to burn, she supposed.

But the *bones*. They were always the last to go, yet nothing remained.

*What do you think, that he got out? The door locks from the outside.*

She was being dumb. Candy's paranoia was getting to her. Jeez, the girl was *so* frightened of this place. Not a normal fear, the way some people are afraid of bugs or snakes. This was more of a paralyzing terror. What caused it? Something in Candy's past? Or had she genuinely seen someone down here?

Well, perhaps they could exchange stories over drinks tonight. That's what people did on dates, right? She thought so. Sandra had never been on a date before. It was funny how it took a nightmare situation like this to finally bring her close to someone. With nowhere to hide, she had let her feelings out, and Candy had responded in kind. Hadn't she? Sandra sloshed the mop in the bucket and fantasized about her date with Candy. In her mind, she was witty and charming, always saying the right thing, and when their hands brushed together, she felt an electric spark between them. She imagined them in bed, exploring each other's bodies.

Unexpectedly, she cried. What was this sensation she felt? Happiness? She remembered being happy as a child, even as a teenager. But then it had been taken from her.

*Stop bringing yourself down.*

But she always did. Happiness was fleeting, joy short-lived.

Sighing, she lifted the mop. The water dripped steadily onto the floor.

She looked around for where to start, and saw there was no blood.

*Anywhere.*

There were two sets of dusty footprints, and a small indentation from where the priest's body had lain... but no *blood.*

"Huh," said Sandra. She sniffed and wiped away the tears, remembering how the sheet had been soaked in crimson fluid. There was no way it wouldn't have left a mark. Had Martha been down here after all? No, that made no sense. She had specifically told Sandra to come down here and clean up.

She placed the mop back into the bucket. Martha must have forgotten, that was all. The woman had a lot on her mind, and understandably so.

"Well, that was easy," said Sandra. She started to move, then stopped.

*Drip.*

*Drip.*

What was that sound? It wasn't the mop, the head of which was submerged in the bucket.

*Drip. Drip.*

She checked the furnace, then looked up at the ceiling. The bulb hung uselessly, reflecting flames that made it look like a candle.

*Someone really ought to change that bulb,* thought Sandra.

*Drip. Drip.*

It had to be a leak. She remembered the time the sewage pipe had burst, flooding the basement in piss and shit. The smell lingered for months, no matter how many air fresheners and candles they sacrificed to the god of stench.

"That was gross," she muttered, turning towards the door, her eyes catching the fallen crucifix.

She froze.

"What the fuck...?"

Blood.

It dripped from the fingers of the wooden Jesus. His hand was clenched over the edge of the beam, a rusted nail sticking out through the cracked and weathered wood.

A thin red trail ran from the nail, over the curve of the knuckles, and fell into a shallow pool below the cross.

*No, wait...*

She blinked. It had to be a mistake, an optical illusion...

Sandra took a cautious step closer to the carving. She crouched, watching as the scarlet pool seemed to quiver in anticipation. A bubble formed in the center of the pool, the small droplet rising from the liquid, shooting up towards the effigy's hand.

The blood was dripping *up*.

It wasn't possible. Sandra stared, scarcely able to believe her eyes. What was that word she had learned about in church, that religious miracle? Stigmata? Was that it?

"In a whorehouse basement," she whispered.

The pool bubbled, and another droplet emerged, flying through the air towards the figure's curled fingers. Except now the fingers stretched out, reaching for the blood, *straining* for it.

"Jesus," she said, leaping to her feet and staggering backwards. She felt the heat from the furnace on her back. "That's not—"

Two hands clamped down on her shoulders. The pain was immense, a savage burning sensation. She tried to shake free, but they clung on, the withered fingers digging into her flesh, ripping through her skin and scraping against bone.

Sandra screamed. The hands kept pulling, until her back touched the hot metal of the furnace and she felt it sizzle. Desperately, she clawed at the hands, but the fingers had burrowed deep into her skin and now gripped onto her collarbones. There was little blood, the immense heat from the burning digits cauterizing the wounds as they appeared.

Her hair caught fire, erupting around her like a halo as melting flesh dribbled down her neck, scalding her. She screamed louder. One of the hands released her clavicle and plunged into her mouth. She choked on the foul appendage as it twisted around, the fingertips sinking into her soft palate, puncturing it, lodging there like a fishing hook.

It lifted her.

Her clothes had burned away, and her skin stuck to the metal, ripping free from her torso as the hands dragged her up, towards the furnace door, towards her doom, her feet leaving the ground, kicking the sides, her neck bending backwards as she reached the hole where she and Candy had disposed of the priest's body.

It was bringing her inside.

The frame of the door scraped against her skinned back, each bone of her spinal column juddering along the lip. The pressure in her head built, and as she felt her tongue and face blacken, and her hair burn like kindling, she opened her throbbing eyes and took one maddening look at the skull of the priest.

The bastard was smiling.

# PART II

DEATH

**11**

———

Three miles away, in Lower Manhattan, Johnny Cruz was leaning against the cemetery wall. He flashed the girl — Yvonne was her name — his famous smile, and cupped his hands together in front of him, entwining his fingers.

"Come on, baby. I'll help you up."

Yvonne giggled. "This is messed up. A cemetery?"

"Why not? It's *dead* quiet."

It was a terrible joke, but Yvonne was so drunk that she laughed anyway. She swayed before him, her brown eyes peering at him from beneath tousled bangs.

"You're just trying to get into my pants," she slurred.

"Baby, you're not even *wearing* pants," he said, gesturing at her knee-length skirt. "So how can I get into your pants?"

It was another howler, and he knew he had labored it by hammering home the punchline, but still the girl laughed. Man, this chick was *wasted*. Johnny smiled. The party had been a dead scene, a bunch of nerds waxing lyrical about films and their power to change the world or some shit. He had only been there looking to score, and Yvonne — the drunkest person in the room, and who had looked as bored as he felt — had seemed the likeliest candidate.

"Come on, put your foot on my hands," he said.

She narrowed her eyes. "You got grass, right? You promised me grass."

"I got *all* the grass. Now hurry up before someone sees us."

She held onto his shoulders to steady herself and raised her foot, placing it on his clasped hands. She had killer legs, Johnny thought.

"Ready?"

She smiled crookedly. "Go for it."

He lifted her. For one perilous second, he thought she would lose her balance and topple backwards onto the sidewalk, but then she was halfway over, hands scrabbling against the brickwork, her legs splayed as she tried to hook one of them over the wall, causing her skirt to ride up to her waist. Johnny grinned as he enjoyed the view.

"Need any help?"

"A little."

He placed his hands on her ass.

"Hey, what are you doing?" she cried.

"Giving you a push."

"Well... *oh, shit!*"

With one shove, she disappeared over the wall, her legs going vertical before vanishing. Johnny grimaced as he heard the thump of her hitting the ground on the other side.

"You okay?"

There was an awkward beat of silence.

"I made it," she said.

A broad grin stretched across Johnny's face. It was amazing how rubbery people were when they were drunk. He took a couple of steps back, then ran at the wall, leaping and grabbing onto the top. His leather boots scratched at the surface, and then he was up, perched atop it like an oversized crow. The girl was flat on her back below him, her skirt still around her waist. She looked up at him and laughed again.

"What are you doing up there?"

"Coming to get you," said Johnny.

She rolled onto her front and got to her feet. "You'll have to catch me first!" She staggered off in a loping run, bouncing merrily off tombstones. Johnny jumped, landing heavily on the grass, and gave chase. It was too easy. He caught up to her in seconds. He grabbed her thin coat and spun her to face him, and she slipped and tumbled to the ground, laughing hysterically.

"The grass is wet," she giggled. "I fell."

"I know, baby. I saw." He sat by her side. She was right. The dew soaked uncomfortably through the seat of his jeans.

"You know, you're real beautiful by starlight," he said.

"I bet you say that to all the girls."

"Just the pretty ones."

He kissed her, and she let him. She tasted of cherries and tequila.

"What about that grass?" she smiled.

"I know, it's wet."

"Not *that* grass, silly. The *grass*."

"In a minute. I wanna kiss you first."

He nuzzled her neck, his hands finding her waist, working their way under her blouse.

"The grass," she said, her voice muffled by his lips and probing tongue.

"Soon."

His fingers slid up her soft belly to her breast. She wasn't wearing a bra, her nipples hardening at his touch as she fumbled inexpertly at his belt buckle. Quickly, she gave up.

"Take them off," she said, leaning back seductively and accidentally cracking her skull off the tombstone.

Johnny shook his head. His attempt to fuck her was descending into farce faster than a Three Stooges film. If she sustained one more head injury, she'd knock herself out cold.

"Here, let me do it," he said, unbuckling his pants. He helped her lie down, then removed his pants and underwear. The wet grass squelched unpleasantly beneath them.

"Your turn," he said as he unbuttoned her blouse.

"Can't I keep my clothes on?"

"Baby, that wouldn't work. Come on, let's do this, then we can have that grass. You're so pretty." He opened her blouse. "My god, your breasts are *magnificent.*"

"I know," she giggled, continuing to do so as he bent forwards and ran his tongue over her nipples. At the same time, he tugged her panties down her thighs.

*Who said men can't do two things at once,* he thought, as he stripped Yvonne's underwear off, leaving the flimsy garment dangling from one ankle.

"Hey, you hear something?" she said.

"Not a thing," replied Johnny. His dick was too hard for him to think. He spread the chick's legs and positioned himself between them.

"No, wait," she said. "I really hear something. What's that noise?"

"Who fucking cares," snapped Johnny, though he heard it too. A strange sound. Something scratching, or... or crumbling. It sounded far off, but when he put his dick into Yvonne and she gasped, he forgot all about it.

Their bodies pressed together, locked in the throes of

lovemaking. Johnny looked down at the girl. In the moonlight, he could see her eyes were closed. He hadn't been lying; she was a very attractive girl. He wondered if he could get her number after—

A long, rumbling groan sounded, like a burst of flatulence from the earth itself.

"That you, baby?" asked Johnny.

"Don't stop," she said, shaking her head and grinding her hips against him.

But Johnny was distracted. The chick was right. There *was* a weird noise. He looked around, then up at the tombstone that towered over them. Was it his imagination, or—

The tombstone moved. It tilted towards them, then stopped. Johnny froze. "Hey, stop," he said. "Don't move."

Yvonne slowed her gyrations. She opened her eyes and stared up at him. "What's wrong? I thought you wanted me?"

Another low rumble from beneath them.

"Oh, shit," said Johnny. "I think the headstone's about to fall on us."

"What?" She tried to wriggle out from under him, and he held her shoulders, pinning her. The earth seemed to crack, and the stone inched forwards.

"Baby, listen to me. *Listen!* We gotta be smart. We move at the same time, okay?"

"Let go of me!" She kicked her feet, and the tombstone tilted another couple of degrees.

"Stop kicking, or we're both gonna die," he said. "Now, listen close. On the count of three, we roll to the left. Together. We roll, and we keep rolling until we're out of its range."

"Okay," she said. She sounded scared. "We roll to the left. My left?"

"No, your right."

"I'm right? We go to my left?"

"No, your right. We go to your right, not left."

"Wait, what?"

"Ah, fuck it, fine. Your left."

The tombstone shifted.

"You ready?" whispered Johnny. Without waiting for an answer, he began to count. "One... two..."

And that was when the ground gave way beneath them.

The turf they lay on seemed to fold over them, as the pair of young lovers tumbled into the dirt. Yvonne smacked off the casket and Johnny landed atop her. Walls of worm-ridden earth poured down alongside them. Yvonne pushed Johnny off, her head darting back and forth, eyes panic stricken.

"Are we in a grave? Are we in a fucking grave?"

They were. Johnny looked around. He saw the sky above them, surrounded by a rectangle of cemetery dirt. It smelled bad. Funky, like... well, like a grave, he supposed. The chick was freaking out. She got up and stood on the slick surface of the casket, her feet sliding out from under her, fingers clawing desperately at the earth.

"Stay cool, baby," he cooed. "I'll get you out."

She wasn't listening to him. He sat up, watching her try to scramble free, her panties still around one ankle, her blouse hanging open. *Shit*. He wasn't gonna get any from *her* tonight. He shuffled away from her to the end of the casket, avoiding the large hole in the top. They must have made it when they landed, he assumed, which would explain the smell. He wondered how long the corpse had been buried here. Would there be anything left of it? Maybe it had some jewelry he could, y'know, *borrow*?

"Help, somebody, please!" screamed Yvonne.

"Pull your fucking panties up," he said. "You look ridiculous."

She turned to him, ready to snap, when her face froze in a rictus of horror. She raised one arm and pointed at him. No, *beyond* him.

He slowly turned around. There was a hole in the earth behind him.

A tunnel.

Dirt cascaded from the top, as if it had been freshly dug.

"What the fuck?"

He squinted into the tunnel. It was pitch black, but...

"What *is* that?"

There was something inside. He heard a scratching sound, as dull, aged nails raked at the mud.

"Jason, move!" screamed the girl.

Had she used the right name, he might have acted faster. But she was drunk, and Johnny spent too long trying to figure out who the hell Jason was. A waterfall of earth cascaded onto the top of his head, and he looked up in time to see the tombstone looming over him.

"Oh shit!" he shouted, and then it fell, obliterating his skull, and as Johnny's body spasmed and died, the thing in the tunnel never once stopped or looked back.

**12**

---

CANDY STEPPED OUT OF THE SHOWER AND WRAPPED A TOWEL around herself. She padded through to the locker room, trying to identify the voices she heard chattering animatedly. It sounded like Beatrice and Paula. Candy didn't know the two girls particularly well, and that was fine with her. She wasn't in a talkative mood.

"Hey, Candy," said Paula.

Candy smiled at her, and Paula resumed gossiping with Beatrice. Apparently, Paula's boyfriend's sister's friend, who lived in Philly, had slept with Mick Jagger after the Stones show, though she had done a ton of coke and wasn't actually sure it was Mick Jagger, or just 'someone who looked like Mick Jagger.' Paula said it had to have been Mick Jagger, because who else looks like Mick Jagger, and Beatrice agreed it must have been Mick Jagger, and Candy desperately wished they would stop using his full name because it was driving her crazy.

She hurriedly applied some makeup in front of the mirror, trying to block the inane conversation out, but her thoughts kept returning to the dead priest, and the man from the basement, so she gave up and listened in. According to Paula's boyfriend's sister's friend, Mick Jagger — or the person who looked like Mick Jagger — had been a great lay, though she had woken up the next morning in the hotel hallway, totally naked and very, very high.

"Living the dream," said Beatrice, and Candy wasn't sure if she was joking or not.

She slipped into Sandra's roommate's blue summer dress. Though a little loose around the bust, it was a better fit than Linda's shorts and vest. Beatrice and Paula stopped talking and gawked at her.

"You finished for the night?" asked Paula.

"No. Got someone waiting."

Beatrice regarded her quizzically. "And you're wearing that? Did he, like, specifically request it? He got a fetish for girls in bland dresses?"

"It's not mine," said Candy. "My clothes are... look, it's a long story."

Paula nodded sagely. "Pooped yourself, huh?"

Candy didn't know what to say to that.

"My brother's uncle did that in a Denny's, once," Paula continued. "Pooped himself. Had to sneak into the back and steal a worker's uniform. They caught him, standing there with his—"

"I didn't..." started Candy, and then gave up. Let them think that. Who cares? She left through the beaded curtain, the girls so engrossed in their conversation that they didn't notice her absence.

In the chilly corridor, Candy shivered. Her hair was still wet. What would her john think? Ah, Joseph wouldn't mind. He was a nice enough guy who had lost his wife a while back in a car accident, and now paid weekly visits to Candy. She figured she bore a vague facial resemblance to the dead woman, because sometimes Joseph called her his wife's name, which was kinda weird if you stopped to think about it, which is why Candy preferred not to.

She glanced down the corridor. The basement door was wide open. Was Sandra still in there? She wanted to see her, to thank her for the dress. Well, just to see her, really. Martha would be pissed, of course. Joseph was waiting for her, and Martha liked things to run on time, but tonight, Martha could go to hell for all Candy cared.

She soon found herself at the basement door, where she waited outside, hovering on the periphery.

"Sandra? You down there?"

Her calls were met with silence, so she poked her head around the door frame.

"Sandra?"

She walked tentatively through the doorway, crossing the threshold, and hesitated.

"Sandra? It's Candy. You there?"

There was light coming from the basement. It didn't reach the stairs, but there *was* light.

A shadow moved.

"Is that you?"

No answer. Who else could it be?

She put her foot on the first step.

*One.*

The coldness hit her, the temperature dropping rapidly.

The shadow by the furnace was definitely a figure. It was hunched over, long hair obscuring the profile.

She took the next step.

*Two.*

"Sandra?"

*You can do this. Just eight more.*

"Oh, fuck this," said Candy. It couldn't be Sandra. The

girl would have replied by now. Candy turned, heading for the door, and someone was there, waiting, the terror from the basement, the nightmare—

"Where the hell have you been?" asked Paula. She leaned theatrically against the door frame. "Martha's had me and Bea running all over the place looking for you."

Candy waited for her pulse to slow, her hand pressed to her heart. Feeling unsafe, she slipped past Paula into the corridor, leaving the cold air and strange atmosphere of the basement behind.

"I was looking for Sandra," she said. "I've only been gone a minute."

"Are you kidding?" Paula checked her watch. "You've been gone at least a half hour."

"Bullshit," breathed Candy. "I was—"

Paula held her skinny wrist up, showing Candy the digital display. It meant nothing to Candy. She had no idea what time she had left the two girls gossiping.

"Look, Martha's on the warpath. You'd better go, pronto. You think Sandra's down there?" she said, gesturing into the basement.

"Yeah, maybe," said Candy, still confused. She couldn't possibly have been gone thirty minutes. How long had she stood on those steps?

"Cool," said Paula. "I've got to find her too." She paused, then murmured, *"Because apparently that's what I do now."*

Candy's heart rate was returning to normal. She took several deep breaths as Paula watched her curiously.

"You okay?" asked Paula. "You look like shit."

"I'll be fine. I *am* fine."

With that, she walked towards the waiting room, leaving Paula at the top of the basement stairs. She was aware of the girl's eyes on her back, and it made her self-conscious. Part of her wanted to wait and see if Paula located Sandra, but now she was way behind schedule, and Martha would be livid.

She arrived at the door to the waiting room. Pungent cigar smoke wafted out in thick gray clouds. Before entering, she pulled the blue dress down to reveal her cleavage, licked her lips, and counted down from three.

*Sexy. You've gotta be sexy. Forget about everything else that's happened tonight, and go earn your rent.*

She sidled into the room, where several impatient-looking men sat. Joseph was on the pink sofa, chatting with Linda. They both looked up at her as she entered.

"Sorry to keep you waiting," she purred, and beckoned Joseph forth with her finger, effortlessly slipping back into work mode. Joseph stood, and she took his hand and led him from the room without another word.

As they headed for the stairs, she glanced a final time down the corridor, hoping to see Sandra and Paula walking towards her.

But there was no one there, no one and nothing but endless, pitiless darkness, and somewhere, buried within, lay the basement, so cold and dreadful.

Paula lurked in the doorway, watching Candy take her john by the hand and lead him up the stairs. When Candy paused and looked towards her, Paula raised a hand and waved, but the girl mustn't have seen her. A few seconds later, she was gone, and Paula was alone.

She pulled a cigarette from the carton nestled between her breasts. Something had spooked Candy. Bad. The girl looked terrified. But the basement had that effect on people, for reasons Paula could never put her finger on. Sure, it was dark, and it smelled funky, and there were rats and spiders… but that was no different to the subway toilets at the nearest station. At least the basement didn't have any rapists or killers skulking in it.

"Hey, Sandra, you down there? Martha's looking for you."

All was quiet. The whole *building* was quiet tonight, and if it stayed that way, it was gonna be a rough one. No johns meant no pay, and, most importantly, no tips. It wasn't as if Martha was paying them a fucking salary. The price of everything kept going up. Paula already lived with three roommates, all working girls. If rent continued to rise, they would have to find a fifth sucker to sleep in the closet.

"Time to net myself a sugar daddy," she said, only half-jokingly.

She looked down the stairs. A cruel smile crossed her lips as she remembered the initiation ceremony they used to give the new girls when they started working for Martha. They would take them into the basement, strip them naked, and tie them to the old wooden crucifix as if they were fucking the rotten Jesus. They would leave the screaming girls there overnight and come back in the morning, and any chick that wished to stay after that ordeal was welcomed into the fold. Martha had made them stop the ceremony after the unfortunate rat incident of seventy-nine, which had cost the boss a lot of cash in hush money.

She flicked the light switch. Nothing happened.

"How many hookers does it take to change a lightbulb," she said, and started down the stairs. They groaned beneath her.

"Sandra?"

There was no answer. She considered turning back. The

furnace door was open, and a fire roared inside. It cast a flickering light over the basement, illuminating it in all its decrepit glory. Martha should have gotten rid of all the old church stuff years ago. If that shit went up in flames, in a building with no windows and only two exits, then...

Something caught her eye.

The cross. It lay on its side, propped up against the badly stacked pews where it had always lived. But this time, there was something different about it.

The wooden Jesus... it was *gone*.

"Well, that's fucking weird," said Paula. Who the hell would steal *that*? It was a horrible thing, twisted and warped, with painted red eyes that seemed to follow you. It was why it was so effective for the initiation ceremonies — it was fucking *nightmarish*.

Had someone turned the cross around? She walked closer, checking the other side. Nothing. There were holes in the wood where the Jesus had been attached by nails, holes that were jagged and splintered like the carving had been rudely torn off. And recently too, judging by the freshness of the wound.

The wound?

Paula forced a smile. For the first time, she understood why some of the girls were so afraid to set foot in here. She felt a chill. It coiled around her like an unwanted lover, panting nightmarish nothings in her ear.

She looked at the furnace. Had Martha used it for firewood?

"Bitch, you are going straight to hell," said Paula, but the joke alleviated little of the tension. Fuck it. She wanted out of here. Sandra was probably back now, cracking her little leather whip and pissing into some guy's mouth, or whatever it was she did.

Paula turned away from the furnace, from the empty cross, and then she saw it.

The figure.

It lurked in the far corner of the room, a strange and shapeless silhouette lit by the spitting fire. It faced the wall, kneeling as if in prayer.

"Uhhh... Sandra?"

It looked like a girl. She was naked, and blood trickled down her pale skin. Paula flashed back to that ill-fated morning in seventy-nine when she had found the new initiate strapped to Jesus and covered in rats, their sharp teeth nibbling on her flesh, blood gushing from wounds all over her nude body.

She pushed the mental image aside and took a step towards the person in the corner.

"Sandra?"

*Shit, shit, shit. What now? Martha's gonna hit the fucking roof.*

Another step closer.

"Are you okay?"

The naked girl turned her head, staring at Paula through unkempt hair that covered her face like ragged curtains. Something soft flapped in her hands. It reminded Paula of an uncooked steak.

If only it *had* been.

Instead, she realized it was skin. A face.

Sandra's *face.*

"Oh god," said Paula.

The hunched figure stood with agonizing slowness. There was something behind it. A body, a *corpse,* a blood-soaked atrocity, the skin missing, the glistening muscle exposed, hints of bone between the gristly sinew and pink, meaty flesh.

Bile rose in Paula's throat. "I'm sorry," she said. "I... I didn't see anything. I'm going, okay?"

The thing let Sandra's loose facial skin fall to the basement floor with a revolting *splat*. Two long nails protruded from its hands, blood dripping steadily from the tips, and only then did Paula understand where the wooden Jesus had gone.

"No," she said, and then the furnace door slammed shut and all went dark.

Fighting the urge to scream, Paula listened. What else was there to do? Maybe she was dreaming, or hallucinating, or having a bad trip, or—

A single wet footstep chilled her blood. Another followed soon after.

Then another.

It was coming closer. It was coming for *her*. With no light to guide her, Paula turned and ran. Where were the stairs? Where the fuck were the—

She smacked into something. A metal cabinet. Her mind raced. The cabinet... okay, okay, that meant the steps should be to her right.

More footsteps. The pace quickening.

Paula felt along the wall, her fingers groping madly.

Suddenly, breathing — which she had managed to do every second of her whole entire motherfucking *life* — was difficult. She stumbled along until her feet struck something. The steps? Yes!

She hurried up them in a deranged rush. Once, she tripped and fell, skinning her knees.

*Skinned. Sandra had been skinned.*

Ignoring the pain, she resumed her manic ascent. Almost there, almost... there...

Her fingers touched the cool metal of the door. They found the handle, turned it, rattled it.

It wouldn't budge.

"Come on!" she hissed. She balled a fist and pounded it against the door. "Help me! *Help!*"

She tried the handle again. Useless. She hammered the door with both hands, kicked it.

"I'm in the basement! Please, someone help me!"

Where *was* everyone? Why was no one coming to her aid?

Her fists loosened, and she leaned her forehead against the metal and cried, slapping the door with her palms.

"Please," she sobbed, waiting for the nightmare creature to catch up to her, to kill her and skin her like it had done to Sandra.

So she waited.

And waited.

And waited some more.

With aching weariness, Paula turned her head and looked back down the stairs. It was too dark to see anything. The footsteps had stopped, and now all she could hear was her own breathing.

"Oh my god," she panted. Afraid to move, she simply stood there, immobile, for what felt like days. The darkness pressed in around her, and though she knew the basement was a decent sized room, claustrophobic panic nagged at her. With trembling hands, she reached into her top and found the cigarette carton. From inside, she pulled a lighter. The carton slipped from her hands and hit the wood, but she didn't dare pick it up. Not until she could see. She flicked the wheel. The lighter sparked but did not catch.

"Come on," she said, and tried again.

The flame erupted, and there, *there* it was, the thing wearing Sandra's skin. But somehow, that wasn't the worst part of it. It was the eyes. Where they should have been were two inky pits of lunatic nothingness, the dearth of humanity, the utter, abject absence of a *soul*. Its thin arms were raised, the long, rusted nails embedded in its withered hands poised to strike.

Paula barely had time to scream before the points punctured her throat from either side. She had the brief sensation of the two nails scraping together inside her, and saw a foul gout of blood shooting from her neck, before her eyes closed for the last time, and once more all was quiet in the whorehouse basement.

**13**

———

Outside, the rain was starting to fall.

Officer Herman Colt parked the cruiser and glanced at his partner. Officer Maroney took a bite of his meatball sandwich, wrapped the remains in a napkin, and stuffed it down the side of the seat for later. It was a habit that drove Colt crazy, but he had given up on reprimanding the younger officer. Life was too fucking short.

"It's raining," Maroney said.

"Yup," replied Colt. "So it is." He drummed his fingers gracelessly off the wheel and glanced out the window at the cemetery. The perimeter walls hid most of the graves from view, but some of the taller constructions were visible against the night sky. Colt couldn't imagine anything more tragic than being buried in the middle of a city. He had spent his entire existence trying to get away from the constant din of New York City, and the idea of spending the afterlife wandering heaven searching for earplugs was worse than death itself.

"No one else here," said Maroney, wiping his grease-stained fingers on his pants and interrupting Colt's thoughts.

"Yeah. Looks like we're first on the scene."

"Shit. Wanna circle the block and see if someone arrives before us?"

Colt did, but his conscience — or what remained of it after thirty years of police work — got the better of him. Well, that and the fact that some old fart with a pronounced limp was hurrying towards them and waving his hands.

"Look at this asshole," said Maroney. Colt grunted and stepped out onto the street, slamming the door behind him.

"You boys took your damn time," said the man as he approached, the rain thrumming off his checked lumberjack coat.

"Busy night, pops," said Colt. "You the gravedigger?"

"Caretaker," replied the man proudly.

"A yes or no will suffice, sir."

The man looked disappointed. "In that case, yes." He wiped rain from his eyes and squinted at the officers. "She's still in the grave. Can't get her out for love nor money."

"Is she dead?"

"No. He is, though. He's as dead as they come." The caretaker chuckled and headed towards the gate. "Follow me, I'll show ya."

Colt glanced at Maroney and shrugged. "After you."

"Heard her screaming, poor girl," the gravedigger was saying. "All my life, I ain't never heard screams like it. Course, in my line of work, you don't expect to hear screaming, know what I mean? My colleagues are nice and quiet, just the way I like 'em." He pointed ahead of him. "This way. Row thirty-six."

As they walked, Colt glanced around. The headstones

were in poor shape. Many were broken, or defaced with graffiti. Others leaned forwards, or tilted at surprising angles.

"Thought you said you were the caretaker?" said Colt.

"That I am, sir. Have been for forty years." He stopped and glared at Colt. "Why'd you ask?"

Colt put his hand on a headstone and tried to shove it back into position. "Because it doesn't look like you've been taking great *care* of the place."

The old man nodded, his brow furrowing thoughtfully. "Yeah," he grunted. "It's the damnedest thing. Wasn't like this an hour ago."

"What do you mean?" asked Colt, but the man had resumed walking.

"She's over here. See if you can get any sense out of her. Damn kids, with their PCP. Shouldn't have been in here. I locked up at six on the dot, like I'm s'posed to." He looked over his shoulder at Colt. "I take my work seriously, officer." He turned away again. "Right over here."

Colt followed. He heard the girl before he saw her. She was sniveling, mumbling, crying, like a junkie needing a fix. Standing on the edge of the grave, he peered in, and there she was, hugging her legs, knees up at her chin, her pink undergarments around one ankle. Colt produced a flashlight from his pocket and shined it into the girl's face. She didn't respond, didn't even seem to notice. Colt trailed the beam of light along the grave, searching for—

"Shit," he said. He looked at Maroney. "Well, this is a new one for me."

The girl's boyfriend — he assumed it was her boyfriend — lay across the casket. A headstone rested on his upper torso. It had flattened him, forcing some of his insides *outside.* Colt was almost impressed. Every time he thought he had seen it all, the city hurled some new atrocity at him. Crushed by a headstone while fucking in an open grave. He didn't relish the idea of explaining *that* to the kid's parents.

"I'll radio for an ambulance," said Maroney.

"Better make it a meat wagon," said Colt.

Maroney took a last look at the carnage, shook his head, and walked back towards the cruiser.

Colt scratched at his neck. The rain was getting heavier, the grave filling with water. "Why was this one open?" he asked, addressing the caretaker without looking at him.

"Oh, it wasn't. That's the grave of Reginald Bartleby, and he was buried in the year of our Lord nineteen-seventy-two."

"So what are you telling me, pops? That these kids snuck in and dug it up themselves?"

"I never said that."

"So what happened? It just collapsed?"

"Must've done. Bad soil."

Colt looked wearily at the man. "Bad soil? That's the best you got?"

"You got a better idea, *officer?*"

Colt didn't appreciate his tone. "Yeah, I do, matter of fact. I think maybe an unprofessional gravedigger isn't doing his job properly. What'd you do, half-fill in the grave, then put a layer of turf over the top?"

The man snorted. "This ain't my handiwork, no sir. I didn't bury this poor asshole. If I had, this never woulda happened. These younger fellas, to them it's just a job. A way to make money. But I take pride in my work, always have."

Colt nodded. He hadn't asked for the old man's life story. "So what do *you* think happened? Other than bad soil?"

"Earthquake," said the gravedigger.

"Earthquake?"

*"Earthquake."*

"Been no reports."

The gravedigger shrugged, and both men turned their eyes back to the girl.

"Can *you* tell me what happened?" he asked. She continued mumbling, the rain plastering her hair to her forehead. "Thought not," said Colt. She was clearly in shock, and would be no use to him now. Or possibly ever.

A scream cut through the night.

*"Shiiiit!"*

Colt recognized his partner's voice and spun, his hand dropping to his regulation firearm. Rain battered his face as he scanned the cemetery, seeing nothing but crooked head-stones and leafless trees swaying in the wind. He took a step forwards, readying his pistol.

"What in the *shit* is that?" he heard the gravedigger say, and then he saw it with his own eyes, a sight that sent a tremble through his limbs, as fear, the likes of which he had never known, gripped him.

Two hands emerged from the ground, pale and wet and streaked with mud. They clawed at the air, then clamped onto the grass.

"It's a goddam zombie," said the gravedigger.

Colt aimed his pistol, placing his free hand on his forearm to steady his aim.

A head appeared from the grave.

"Aw, shit, Colt. Don't shoot!" said Maroney.

Colt drew in the deepest breath of his life and lowered his service weapon. "What the fuck are you doing?"

"Damn ground just fell away." He held his hands out. "Hey, help me out, would ya? Stinks in here."

Colt turned to the gravedigger. "Earthquakes, huh? *Zombies?* You've got some explaining to do, old timer, and you'd better spin me the greatest story ever told or I'll make sure that by Monday you'll—"

"I already *told* you, it's nothing to do with me. I never dug either of these graves. Not a one in this whole section."

Colt sighed, ignoring Maroney's cries for assistance. Why was nothing ever straightforward? "Okay then," he said. "Then humor me. Who *did* dig those graves?"

"The city," he said.

"The *city.*"

"That's right. The city. They paid for it, arranged the whole thing. Brought some crew in, let them take over my cemetery for two weeks. I was pissed, I'll tell you that."

Colt felt a headache building. "Okay, fine. But why?"

"Because, like I told you, I take pride in my work. I wasn't about to let—"

"Not why were you *pissed,* you stupid asshole. Why did the city hire a team to dig some goddam graves?"

"Well, it was a big job, I guess. Too big for one man, that's what they said."

"I swear to God, if you don't—"

"You remember that church that burned down about a decade back, up by the Hudson?"

"The Manhattan Riverfront." Colt remembered it well. He had been there that first night, preventing gawking civilians from getting too close. "What about it?"

The man grinned. "That's what I'm trying to tell you. When that yahoo from the west bought the land and built that damned useless factory, they had to relocate the bodies from the churchyard."

"What's your point?"

This time the man laughed a full, hearty belly-laugh. "NYPD's finest, huh?" He stopped smiling when he saw the look on Colt's face. "It's simple. This area here — this exact area where we're standing — is where they moved the bodies to."

**14**

———

"Oh yeah, you're good, you're so good," purred Candy as Joseph pounded his cock in and out of her. His body had tensed, and his hands gripped her buttocks like he was juicing an orange. She stared up at the ceiling, counting the cracks and waiting for him to finish.

"Uh," said Joseph, his face buried in her neck, his teeth against her skin. "Uh!"

"Don't give me a hickey," she said sharply. He pulled back, then started to lick her, lapping her cheek with his wet tongue, reminding Candy of an overeager dog.

His hands found her face and turned it towards his, and he kissed her on the lips, and she kissed him back because he had paid her to do so, and she trusted him to understand it was all part of the transaction.

Candy moaned with fake pleasure. They had been going at it for close to half-an-hour now, and still he seemed no closer to coming. She had faked an orgasm three times already, and her pussy was sore. She made a mental note to take some painkillers as soon as Joseph was done. His movements slowed, and she smacked his ass because she knew he liked that, but instead of ejaculating, he rolled off her and sat on the edge of the bed, his head bowed.

Candy stared at his back, at the subtle curve of his spine. The silver chain he always wore around his neck had spun round during their session, and the little metal crucifix was turned towards her.

"Wow, you made me come so hard," she lied. "I'm wiped out."

He snapped the empty condom off and let it dangle from his hand. "Thanks."

Sensing something was wrong, she got to her knees and went to him, draping her arms over his shoulders and pressing her breasts against him. "Hey, you okay? Was it not good for you?"

He turned his head and kissed her softly. "No, it was amazing. *You* were amazing. As always." He looked away. "Sorry I told you I love you. I get... confused, sometimes. Say, you hurt yourself?"

She realized he was staring at the cuts on her arm. "I'm fine. Attacked by a grizzly bear."

"In New York?" he smiled.

"Yeah. You should see *him,* though. Doctors say he'll never play piano again."

Joseph laughed. "What a tragedy."

"Big time." She lightly massaged his shoulders. "You okay?"

"Sure. Why?"

She pointed at the condom. "Because that thing's not usually empty. You want to try something else? I can use my hands, or my mouth?" It was never good to leave a client unsatisfied. Especially one that tipped well. Repeat business from reliable men was the only sure thing in sex work.

"Nah, not tonight," said Joseph. "Got a lot on my mind.

Work's tough, and… and I have a date on Saturday. My first one since… well, let's just say my first date in a long time."

"Wow. Who's the lucky girl?" asked Candy, as she slid across the bed to retrieve her dress.

"A woman I met at the gym. Name's Kirsten. She seems nice."

"I hope it goes well."

It was true, she did wish him well, though she didn't want to lose one of her best and most regular johns. It was inevitable, she supposed. Joseph was a handsome guy, with a toned body and adorable, floppy hair like a kid. He also had a huge cock, though his knowledge of a woman's erogenous zones was as poor as most of the men that passed through.

*He just needs a good teacher,* she thought. She wondered if she would have been attracted to him had she been straight.

Joseph deposited the condom in the trash and started to dress. Diana Ross was singing *Upside Down* on the radio as Candy reached for her cigarettes.

"Want one?"

"No thanks," said Joseph. He was always in such a hurry to leave, like he was embarrassed or ashamed about what he'd done.

He took out his wallet and counted out fifty bucks, laying it on the bed. That was for the kissing. Then he produced another twenty as an extra. "I got a bonus this month," he said by way of explanation.

"Thanks, honey. I'll see you next week, right?"

"Probably," he muttered. "At least I know *you* won't reject me."

Candy picked up the money and walked over to him. Normally she wasn't in the mood for a heart-to-heart with her johns, but she wanted to take her mind off what had gone down earlier.

*You're gonna have to sleep sometime. And when you do, you'll have nothing but time to think.*

She shoved the thought aside.

"If this Kirsty—"

"Kirsten," he interrupted.

"Okay, if this Kirsten rejects you, then she wasn't worth knowing." She took him by the arm and they left the room, waking together towards the stairs. "You're a good guy."

"It's just, I haven't done this in so long. I don't know what to say to women."

"You know what to say to me."

"That's different."

They started down the stairs.

"It is, and it isn't," she said. "Yes, you're paying to spend time with me. But I'm just a normal woman too. I'm no different from Kirsty—"

"Kirsten."

She glanced at him, and he laughed.

"I'm no different from *Kirsten,*" she said. "Talk to her the way you're talking to me now. Don't put her on a pedestal. Just be yourself. Be kind. And if all else fails, show her how big your dick is."

He smiled at that, the way all men do when they've been complimented on their penises.

"Man," he said, "I wish I could meet a girl like—"

"Don't even say it," she said. "I never mix business with pleasure, you know that."

They reached the bottom of the stairs and passed the waiting room. Candy glanced in. There were a couple of johns lounging on the chairs — one of them was Hart, one of Foxy's regulars — and the front-of-house girl Daniella was serving them drinks. Christ, they must really be running behind schedule tonight if Martha was plying them with alcohol. Booze cost money, and Martha was in the sex trade to *make* money, not spend it, or so she liked to say.

Candy and Joseph arrived at the big metal double doors.

"Look, you relax and have a good time on Saturday, okay?"

"I will. I'll promise."

"And if you take her to bed, try not to think of me."

He reached for one of the doors and grabbed the handle, pulling it open. "Ha, well now you've put the idea in my head, how can I—"

The door clanged violently to a stop.

At first, Candy thought he had done something wrong. The door had thumped off his foot, or he was pulling when he should be pushing. But when she looked closer, she realized what the issue was. She took a step backwards.

"Oh shit."

The doors were open just wide enough to see the chain that had been wrapped around the outside handles. She reached through the narrow gap — there was only enough room to get her arm out — and touched the links. They were an inch thick.

Joseph yanked on the handles, but the door was going nowhere. "Who did this?"

Candy brought her arm back in and peered through. It had to be the protestors. Those wackos. But where were they? There was no one around. What were they planning? To set fire to the place? To burn it down like their beloved church and kill everyone inside?

"The back door," she said. "Hurry."

Daniella appeared in the doorway of the waiting room.

"What's that noise?" she asked in a thick Italian accent, but there was no time to explain.

Candy raced down the corridor, Joseph in pursuit. It was dark, but as long as she kept going in a straight line, she'd be okay. As she passed the basement door, she felt the temperature plummet. She didn't stop.

"Who did this?" repeated Joseph, his footsteps echoing alongside her own.

Candy didn't answer. From the far end of the corridor, she heard metal rasping against metal.

Not far now. If she hurried, she could still stop them.

Voices, laughter, a chain pulled taut.

She reached the door and barged it open. In her panic, she caught glimpses of the protestors, their signs and placards lying on the ground, rain smearing the obscene messages.

"There's one of them!" someone shouted, and the group advanced. Candy backed into the doorway as two men came for her, shoving her. She lost her footing and tumbled backwards into the corridor. Jospeh caught her and moved her aside.

"What the hell are you doing?" he said, stepping out into the rain and going toe-to-toe with the first man. Joseph had a good three inches on him. His hands clenched into tight fists.

The loose chain swung from the handle. A couple of women raced towards the door, trying to close it. Out of pure instinct, Candy stepped forwards and put her foot in the way, her lack of shoes never even crossing her mind.

Her foot crunched between the metal door and the frame. The women pulled the door back, alleviating the pressure, and then slammed it again. Bones ground against each other. Candy wanted to scream, but the breath had been sucked out of her. She saw Joseph swing a punch. The first man went down hard, but another was coming. A woman in a pale green church dress leaped onto Joseph's back, clawing at his eyes with raking fingers. Candy leaned against the door to open it further.

Joseph flipped the woman over. She splashed into a puddle and lay there, unmoving. Poor Joseph. He was too slow. He never saw the other man coming, the one with the chain.

"Look out!" cried Candy.

Joseph turned as the chain struck him full force in the face. There was a loud crack as several bones broke. He dropped to his knees, clutching at his face, at the wide hole where his cheek should have been. Blood gushed from the wound, and the chain came down again, this time on his cranium.

It, too, offered no resistance.

He hit the ground, the top of his scalp missing, and Candy swore she could see the white of his broken skull framing the damaged gray of his brain matter.

"No!" she screamed, forcing the door open in a burst of manic adrenaline. She stepped out, ignoring the bruising agony in her foot, and faced the protestors.

They turned as one towards her.

Three men and two women. She glanced down the alleyway. More of them lurked in the shadows. A woman spoke. She wore a red gown, a mink stole draped around her neck.

"The time is nigh," was all she said.

They came for her, and Candy did the only thing she could do to stay alive. She ran back inside. As she did, peals of laughter rang in her ears, and then the door slammed shut for the last time, the chain dragged through the handle.

Now, there was no way out.

**15**

———

DEAD.

Joseph was dead, and *they* had killed him.

Candy staggered into the wall. "Why are you doing this?" she shouted. "Why?"

No one answered. She took a step, putting all her weight on her damaged foot, her eyes closing in agony. She had to move, had to warn the others, and as she limped along the corridor, her hand pressed to the wall for support, she thought it had never looked longer, nor darker. Ahead, she focused on the light of the waiting room, a beacon of sanity in the freakish gloom.

They had killed once. They would surely kill again. Joseph had done nothing to deserve that. Unless they somehow knew about the priest? Were they aware that he was dead, and that she had killed him? How could they be? It was impossible. Absolutely impossible.

She winced as her foot pressed uncomfortably against the floor. God, she was making slow progress. She hadn't even reached the basement yet.

Ahead of her, someone was walking along the corridor.

She raised her hand, prepared to call out, but when she saw the way they moved, a deep, primordial unease from within prevented her.

The person was grotesquely emaciated, like they had been stretched on a medieval torture device, their limbs gangly and overextended, causing them to walk in an unco-ordinated fashion that reminded Candy of a baby giraffe. Were they coming towards or away from her? She waited, watching. It was hard to tell.

Away.

They were walking away from her. So where had they come from?

The basement?

Frozen with horror, she watched in silence as the figure lurched awkwardly down the corridor. In each hand, it held something long and thin. Spikes? Candy couldn't tell. She was too far away, and the lighting was mercifully inade-quate. All she knew was that it was safer to remain in the shadows. The figure resembled the thing she had seen in the basement too closely.

She waited for the nagging, insistent voice in her head to tell her she was crazy... but the voice had been rendered mute.

The sinister figure reached the end of the corridor and turned up the stairs. Then, it was gone. Candy stood a while longer, waiting for the dreadful pounding of her heart to subside, then resumed her journey. She tried to hurry, ignoring the pain in her foot and passing by the basement door without realizing it.

Rambunctious voices drifted from inside the waiting room. Martha's boomed above everyone else, but she sounded different to her usual bullish nature. Almost apologetic?

*"I'm sorry,"* Martha was saying. *"The girls will be here shortly."*

*"This is no way to run a business,"* complained one man. *"It's ridiculous."*

"Martha!" shouted Candy.

*"See? There's one of them now,"* she heard Martha say. *"I'll even take five dollars off as an apology for the inconvenience."*

*"I think your girls need some discipline,"* said another man.

*"What you do with the girls is up to you. Just don't leave any permanent marks."*

Candy opened the door and stumbled inside. She dropped to her knees in front of Martha. The woman stood with her hands on her hips.

"Where the fuck have you been?" she said.

"It's Joseph, they—"

Martha struck her with an open hand.

"Don't talk back to me! I can't find you, I can't find Sandra, I can't find..." She paused, glaring at Candy, looking her up and down. "What the fuck is the matter with you?"

"They killed him," she managed to say. "They killed Joseph."

"Who?" She leaned in close, whispering in Candy's ear. "After what you've been through tonight, if this is some kind of joke..."

"The protestors. They've locked us in. Joseph, he... he tried to stop them." She had been fighting back tears, but now they flowed uncontrollably. "They killed him."

Martha looked dubious. One of the men laughed nervously.

"Go check the front door if you don't believe me," sobbed Candy.

"Is she for real?" asked another man. Candy looked

around at them. Four men and Daniella, the Italian waiting room girl, each eyeing her suspiciously.

Daniella snickered behind her hand. "See boys? You could have had *me* instead," she said in her exaggerated accent.

"Wait here," said Martha to no one in particular. She pushed past Candy and left the room.

"You said someone's dead?" asked one of the men. Hart, Foxy's regular, a tall, bald Black man who was built like a tank.

She nodded, then heard the loud reverberation of the chain tightening against the front doors.

"Listen, I've gotta get outta here," said another man. Candy had slept with him a couple of times before, but she couldn't remember his name. Mikey, or Mickey, or something similar. "My wife'll be home in an hour."

"My shift starts at eleven," said another. "I can't call in and say I'm stuck in a fucking whorehouse."

They didn't seem to understand. This wasn't simply some minor inconvenience they would have to explain to their spouse or boss. A man was dead. A man was fucking *dead*.

Martha reappeared at the door. For once, she looked flustered.

Without glancing at Candy, she took a deep breath and addressed the room.

"Gentlemen," she said. "It appears we have a problem."

**16**

———

Upstairs, Foxy sat naked on the bed and lit a smoke.

Her client lay by her side, his head resting on the pillow, snoring soundly.

Foxy smiled to herself. It was the easiest money she would make all week. They had fucked, he came within two minutes, and now he was fast asleep. She didn't feel bad about it, either. After all, that was what he paid for. The man was an incurable insomniac, and, according to him, he slept no more than an hour per night. The only way he could drift off, he claimed, was by having sex.

Of course, he couldn't stay longer than two hours — Martha wouldn't allow it — but any sleep was better than no sleep, he had told her, and Foxy was only too happy to oblige. She hadn't mentioned it to any of the other girls, not even Candy, lest they tried to steal him away. Hell, he was the dream client. A quick ride — always on top, as he occasionally fell asleep *during* sex — and then plenty of free time to smoke or read or just kick back and relax.

She had picked up a second-hand paperback at The Strand the day before, and lifted it from her bag. *The Other* by Thomas Tryon. It looked like a good, spooky one. She took a draw from her cigarette and opened the book. In the dim light of the bedside candle, she spotted a handwritten inscription on the first page.

> *To my dearest Catherine,*
> *One to read on a long*
> *winter night by the fire!*
> *All my love, M.*

She read it, then reread it. There was something about inscriptions in books that always made her curiously sad. Who was this M? A lover? A parent? A friend? The book had been gifted, yet Foxy had found it in a used bookstore. What had happened? Were they a couple that had split up? Or perhaps M had died, and, heartbroken, Catherine had rid herself of the book, unable to bear looking at the loving words.

What could the mysterious M stand for?

Michael? Madeleine?

She decided to keep reading. The clock was ticking, and she hadn't even reached the copyright page.

Her client stirred. "Mmm... wha..." he said.

Foxy knew what to do. With her cigarette burning between her lips, she reached for his cock and ran her fingers up and down the shaft. It grew hard, and, without putting her book down, she continued to stimulate him until he dozed off again.

She remembered her teachers back home who had told her she was worthless and would never amount to anything, and smiled.

*If you could see me now,* she thought.

But she kept returning to the inscription.

*All my love, M.*

Could it be M for Mom? The words reminded her of what her own mother had written in a Sherlock Holmes collection she gave to Foxy when she left home.

*We're all so proud of you.*
*Our little girl, all grown up.*
*Don't forget about us on*
*your big city adventure.*
*Hope to hear from you soon.*
*Love, mom*

She had been the first member of the family to leave their small suburban town and go seek her fortune elsewhere. The day she left, her mother had wept. She had wept during breakfast, she had wept on the drive to the station, and as the bus pulled out of the lot and Foxy waved from the rain-streaked window, her mom had still been weeping.

*Don't forget about us.*

She hadn't. How could she? She loved her family, loved them dearly. So why had she not sent them a letter in two years? No longer feeling like reading, Foxy placed the book on her lap. Her lack of contact with her family was no great puzzle. It came down to one thing.

Embarrassment.

She wasn't *ashamed* of being a prostitute. It was, after all, just a job. But would her family see it that way? Would her mother?

*Our little girl, all grown up.*

It wasn't meant to be like this. She still remembered her first day in her new job as an assistant editor at a publishing house, and the look on her employer's face when she walked in and they realized she was a Black woman. Her interviews had been conducted over the phone, and the interviewer had gushed over Foxy's application. Had they just *assumed* she was white? She thought so. Despite producing what she believed was consistently good work, they let her go after six months. She couldn't prove it was due to the color of her skin — no one had ever been openly racist to her — but suddenly Foxy found herself with no income and, two weeks later, no accommodation. Her landlord kicked her out when she was unable to pay next month's rent, locking the door and keeping Foxy's belongings as payment.

In retrospect, that was when she should have gone home. But the sting of humiliation was too great, and she realized only too late the irony of her pride forcing her to panhandle on the street rather than face her loving family as a supposed failure.

It was Martha who had saved her. An encounter in a bar led to an invitation to work for the woman, initially in exchange for nothing more than a bed to sleep in. Despite the predatory nature of their relationship, Foxy was grateful that Martha had offered her a second chance.

She missed her home, and she missed her family... but she could never go back again. What would she tell them? The truth? At night, she concocted make-believe stories, tales of drug addiction and prison and gang violence, anything to make it appear she had no choice about her lot in life. But she knew that deep down, she *had* chosen to work here. And that sometimes, she even enjoyed it. How could she tell her parents that? They were deeply religious, and though Foxy had never shared their beliefs, she couldn't bear the thought of disappointing them.

But wasn't she disappointing them anyway? Wouldn't they be happy to know she was safe and well? One time, she had visited her old apartment and asked the landlord if he had kept any of the letters her mom had sent to the address. He laughed in her face, and Foxy had knocked him out with a right hook.

She never went back.

A tear rolled down her cheek, and she wiped it away. She looked at the man sleeping next to her, and... wait, what was that?

A faint sound, like the branches of an old tree in the wind.

The door handle.

It was turning. Slowly, very slowly indeed, but turning nonetheless. Who the hell was it? Didn't they know the room was occupied?

*"Hey,"* she hissed, trying to keep her voice down. *"I'm in here."*

Her client groaned softly.

Shit. She didn't want to wake him. Had she locked the door? The handle continued to turn. Her body tensed as it clicked... and the door remained closed. She breathed a heavy sigh.

Then came a knock. Two quick raps, like sharp metal banging against the wood.

"Whaaas tha?" mumbled her client.

Foxy ran her hand through his hair. "Don't worry, baby. I'll take care of it. You sleep."

Then she slid off the bed and padded barefoot across the room. "Who's there?" she whispered harshly. "This room is *taken.*"

There was no reply. Foxy waited, folding her arms across her chest as the cold needled at her bare skin. She put her ear to the door and listened, but the corridor was silent. She glanced at her client and nodded to herself. Crisis averted.

"Dumb bitches," she muttered as she headed back for the—

Two more knocks, as loud as gunshots.

Foxy whirled on her feet and hurriedly unlocked the door, not caring about her nakedness. She wrenched it open.

"Look, I told you…"

But there was no one there. She stepped out into the dim corridor. Christ, it was even colder out here. She shivered and glanced down the hallway. What the fuck? She knew she hadn't dreamed it. The noise had woken her client, dammit. She felt his hand touch her waist, gently caressing her skin.

"I'm sorry they woke you, baby," she said, as she peered into the darkness. There, at the far end of the corridor, she thought she spotted movement. Her client's hand slid around to between her legs, his hard cock probing her ass. "Well," she smiled, closing her eyes and leaning her head back as the man's fingers brushed through her pubic hair. "You want me to send you to sleep again?"

He pulled away, leaving her standing in the hallway.

"So what do you say?" She turned towards him. "Should I…"

She froze.

The man was still in bed, his eyes closed, chest subtly rising and falling. Foxy glanced down over her body, to where only moments before someone's fingers had rested on her vulva. In her periphery, she saw more activity in the shadows of the corridor. A figure, withered and hunched, his bones cracking as he moved.

She looked back towards the bed, but now the room had changed, the peeling white walls replaced with glistening, slime-coated rocks that pulsated like a living, breathing organism. Dozens of arms protruded through the ooze, their fingers twitching spasmodically, reaching for her. Foxy closed her eyes, pressing her palms over them to block out the maddening, impossible vision as thick liquid washed over her feet. She knew what it was without looking. The foul, malodorous stench of blood was unmistakable.

"This can't be real," she whispered.

She was wrong.

The room remained a ghastly purgatory, only now an enormous wooden cross stood sentinel. A woman was attached to it, ancient nails pinning her wrists and ankles to the rotting wood. Aside from a black hood wrapped over her head, she was naked, and covered in black ooze that dripped from the ceiling. To Foxy's horror, the woman was alive and squirming in agony. She attempted to wrest her arms free, but the nails were twisted into a 'U' shape, blood jetting from the wounds.

Foxy slid in the pool of red liquid. A head floated past her, a head that might have once been human but now resembled tenderized meat with two eyeballs. She kicked it away and faced the crucified woman. From all around came ungodly wails and screams, a terrifying cacophony of unbridled, hellish torment.

Hell? Was she in *hell?*

"Help me," said the woman, and though her voice was muffled by the hood that seemed to grow tighter across her face, Foxy recognized it instantly.

Candy.

The blood was rising. It was up to her thighs now, strewn with severed limbs and intestines and unidentifiable masses of tissue and muscle. She waded through it towards her friend.

"I'm coming!" she cried, as beneath the surface, unseen fingers scratched at her legs. She reached the crucifix. Up close, she noticed that the nails protruding from her friend's wrists were *not* nails, but pale, rancid worms, their bodies bloated from gnawing through Candy's pink flesh.

The hood strained across her face, so taut that it resembled a second skin. Foxy reached for it, her fingernails digging into the fabric, tearing it to shreds, ripping it from Candy's hyperventilating face. The women locked eyes, and then Foxy stepped back in horror. Candy's skin undulated, as if a mass of creatures writhed beneath it. One burst through, a fat, white maggot dropping from Candy's cheek. Another pierced her flesh, then another, her eyeballs shriveling like deflated beach balls as more of the insects poured out in an endless, ghoulish torrent. Candy's face drooped, revealing a black, charred-looking skull.

No, not a skull.

A face.

Foxy trembled in fear.

She couldn't run, couldn't even move.

She knew that face.

She had seen it before.

In the basement.

On the crucifix.

On the old wooden Jesus.

Two sharpened points pierced Candy's breasts. The skin stretched and broke, the metal nails rupturing her flesh, pulling it apart, tearing Candy's torso asunder, as the hideous wooden idol stepped out from—

*"Hey, you okay?"*

Foxy felt hands on her body, shaking her, but she was powerless to do anything about it.

*"Snap out of it!"*

A slap stung her cheek, so hard it rocked her head to the side, and when she awoke, she was staring into the sleep-encrusted eyes of her client. She pushed away from him, scrambling backwards until she fell off the bed and landed in a heap on the floor.

"You okay?" he asked.

She looked around at the familiar walls and furniture of the brothel room; at the dusty mirror and flickering candles, at the pile of clothes by the bed, and at her own feet and hands, unstained by blood. It was over. The vision had vanished in the blink of one tear-soaked eyelid.

"You were having a nightmare," her client said, as if she didn't already know. "Must have been a real shitter." He shook his head in disbelief. "You were going *nuts.*"

She put a hand to her cheek, and the man looked ashamed.

"I'm sorry. I had to do it. You weren't waking up."

She gently touched her sore skin. "It's okay," she said, her voice flat, her words stilted. Though the dream was over, the memory remained. "You did what you had to do."

"Thought you were having a seizure at first." The man rubbed at his tired eyes. "Damn, must have been one hell of a dream."

"Yeah. It was." She took a breath. "Sorry I woke you."

He smiled apologetically at her. "Think you can help me sleep again?"

"Sure," she said, despite the lingering sense of dread. "Course I can."

And so she did. Despite her inability to shake the image

of her crucified friend's face bursting open in a flood of maggots, Foxy lay there, pressed against her client's sweaty back, jerking him off until he fell asleep. She tried not to think about the dream.

The nightmare.

The vision.

Whatever it was.

But no matter how hard she tried, she was unable to pinpoint the moment it had begun. The misshapen figure she had witnessed in the corridor. Was *that* real? The knocking at the door? It had to have been. She was awake the whole time.

Once her client had fallen asleep again, Foxy placed the horror novel back in her bag. It no longer felt appropriate. Instead, she sat there, smoking, the cigarette shaking in her hand. She wouldn't be able to sleep. How could she, when she could still smell the blood, and feel the disembodied hands clawing at her?

Foxy started to cry.

God, at the time, it had all felt so real.

It had all felt so *real*.

**17**

———

THREE DOORS DOWN FROM WHERE FOXY LAY TREMBLING IN the darkness, Kelly Martin sat propped up against a mound of pillows. She turned the radio up and began filing her nails, but she could still hear Doc next door in the bathroom.

"Just take a shit before you leave the house," she muttered to herself, as a loud *plop* sounded through the closed door. They would *never* be finished on time. Before they had even started, Sandra — that dumb bitch — had come barreling into the room and taken him away to check on that *other* dumb bitch, Candy, who had fallen and hit her head or something equally stupid.

"You okay in there, honey?" she called to him. She sighed and closed her eyes. "I feel *real* sexy in here. I want your hard co—"

"Just a minute," he interrupted. "It's my IBS."

Kelly bit down on her lip. "Yeah. *Real* sexy," she whispered. The hour he had paid for was almost up, and if she tried to charge him overtime, he'd blame Sandra. Hell, he might charge *them* for his medical services. She didn't know what to do.

"God damn it," she said. The stench was getting worse. How was she supposed to pretend she was into him when the room stank like a dive bar toilet? She got out of bed and crossed to the cabinet in the corner, hoping Linda had left some of her incense in there. The girl was always burning that shit.

"Gotta be something in here," she said, as she rummaged through the sex toys. Dildos, clamps, beads... and there, at the bottom, nestled snugly on top of a pair of crumpled underpants, was a candle. Well, it was better than nothing, she supposed.

A door behind her creaked open.

"That you, hon? Found a candle. Thought I'd create an atmosphere, you know?"

She smiled, pleased at how easily the lie had tumbled from her lips.

The single bulb in the center of the room went out, plunging her into darkness. Jeez, he could have at least let her light the damn thing first.

"Ooh, I like it," she said. "The dark really turns me on." It didn't, actually. But in her line of work, and with some of her less visually appealing clients, darkness was often a welcome friend.

She shuffled back to the bed, careful not to bump her shin against the metal frame, and laid the candle on the bedside table, fumbling for her matches. She knocked her cigarette carton to the floor, grumbled in irritation, then found the matchbook. In spite of the darkness, she managed to strike one, and used it to light the candle. It offered scant illumination.

"You there?" she whispered in her most seductive tone.

Peeling the covers back, she slipped onto the bed. "Look, honey, the clock's ticking, okay?"

Doc grunted through the bathroom door. *"You say something?"*

"Uh, doesn't matter," she replied falteringly.

Huh. She could have *sworn* she'd heard a door open. Or maybe it was the next door down? Sound carried oddly in a building with no windows. Often, it sounded to Kelly like two people fucking next door were in the same bed as her, which she found both concerning and also a little exhilarating. But this felt different. She scanned the room again, but the shroud of darkness was impenetrable except for a thin shaft of light beneath the bathroom door. Kelly shivered. Why did she sense she was not alone in here?

She turned down the radio and listened carefully, at first hearing nothing but Doc's faint moans. Then she identified a second sound. A thin scratching noise, like something scuttling across the floor.

"Who's there?"

Had someone secretly entered? Perhaps some creep, here to take advantage of her? Or a voyeur? She sat alert, waiting for her eyes to adjust, her arms breaking out in gooseflesh. The bed frame groaned, and she felt the mattress rise.

Somebody was under the bed.

*There can't be,* her mind argued. *There's not enough space.*

But that wasn't strictly true. Maybe it was a stray dog? It had happened once before, or so she had been told. What were the odds of it happening again? Slim, she wagered, as she fought the rising tide of fear.

She didn't want to check under the bed. After all, that was where the monsters lived. Everybody knew that. Even her own three-year-old. Of course, *she* didn't believe in monsters anymore. They weren't real. But if they were? Then under the bed is where they would be. It was obvious.

It was a fact.

And so with great reluctance, bordering on mounting hysteria, Kelly Martin leaned over the side of the bed and reached for the yellowing sheets that hung to the floor, obscuring the underneath. She didn't dare get *off* the bed. Monsters may not be real, but there was no sense in tempting fate.

She grabbed the sheet in her shaking fingers, and lifted it partway, revealing a cold, black inch of nothingness. Blood rushed to her head, and she lifted the sheet further, peering into the darkness. As her eyes adjusted, she saw a shape. A figure, its bright white eyes penetrating the tenebrous shadows. She reached her arm under, groping along the floorboards, and found—

She smiled to herself as she pulled out the deflated blow-up sex doll, gazing at its perpetually shocked expression.

"You gave me a scare," she said, before shoving it back under. At that precise moment, Doc ripped a tremendous fart from the bathroom, followed by the contents of his bowels splashing into the bowl.

Kelly laughed. She realized how ridiculous she must look, hanging over the edge of the bed with her bare ass pointing towards the ceiling, and pushed herself back up. She ran her hands through her hair, the tension dissipating like mist on a rainy morning.

"Jeez, control yourself," she said. "It was just a—"

The bed frame shuddered violently.

Kelly's body went rigid. She tried to call out to Doc, but no sound escaped her lips.

The bed sheets were moving.

She glanced down towards her feet, where the sheets were rising as if some unseen intruder was climbing into bed with her. She wanted to scream, but still her mouth opened and closed uselessly, producing nothing but tiny, gasping whimpers. The sheets bulged. It was getting closer. She drew her knees up to her chest, her whole body frozen in abject terror.

"Please," she managed to say, as the sheets drew back and it emerged like a nightmare dragged screaming from the depths of hell, an obscenity, a *horror*. It wore a face on top of its own; a girl's face, torn and savaged and blood streaked.

Kelly opened her mouth and screamed as—

—Doc flushed the toilet.

He gazed into the bowl, at the swirling mass of waste and toilet paper, and patted his belly. The toilet howled, chugging noisily, and he wafted his hands to dispel the stink. If only this damned whorehouse had windows!

He thought he heard a scream over the sound of the flush, but so what? Screams were a common occurrence in a place like this. It just meant the paying customers were getting their money's worth.

*If you don't make a whore scream, you're doing it wrong,* that's what Doc's father used to tell him. He still wasn't entirely sure what the old bastard had meant by that.

"Ah, fuck," he muttered.

The flush hadn't worked. His own shit stared up at him accusingly from the bottom of the filthy bowl. He reached for the chain and pulled again, but the toilet gurgled at him as it slowly refilled. Well, no matter. He could have his way with the girl waiting for him in the bed, and then return to it. He just needed to make sure she didn't use the bathroom.

It wasn't his fault. All women made him nervous, and it played havoc with his insides. Prostitutes were the only women he could even talk to, let alone make love to. He was a different man around them.

Literally.

He had invented his alter ego, Doctor Phillips, the world famous physician, and used the mask of anonymity to regale the ladies with tales of his medical exploits while showering them with tips, which were actually his meagre earnings from driving a cab. One time, he had even picked up one of the girls, and spent the entire journey sinking lower in the front seat, praying she wouldn't recognize him. Earlier that evening, when they had called him to look at that girl who had fainted, he had been sure they would have exposed him as a fraud. Thankfully, the bitch was okay.

He assumed.

She might have had a concussion, but how would he know? He was too distracted by her tits, and the way those tiny shorts disappeared up her snatch.

He felt himself stiffen.

"Yeah," he said, his cock hardening. Next time, he would definitely make sure he got *that* girl. But only if she was wearing those shorts.

Grinning, he pushed open the door, rubbing his dick. The light was off, the room lit only by a candle. Perfect. He could imagine the other girl as he fucked this one. But what the hell was that noise?

There was a wet squelching sound, and something smacking hard off bare skin. Christ, she was fucking someone else on his dime! Angrily, he stalked to the light switch. Had the slut forgotten he was even there? She had some nerve.

He flicked the light on, ready to give her a piece of his mind, and—

There was someone else with her, alright. Someone else in the bed he had paid for.

A thin man, almost skeletal, who perched over Kelly's limp body. Bloody skin sagged from his body, peeling off and revealing a hard brown exterior that resembled old wood. He clutched two long, sharp nails in his hands, bringing them down over and over again into what was left of Kelly's face. There was a sickening crack as bone broke like porcelain. Her breasts had been savaged, fountains of dark blood gushing from the torn and ravaged mounds and soaking into the sheets.

Doc stared, his fingernails scratching the door frame. His bowels loosened again, and he scurried back into the bathroom, but not before releasing one quick, high-pitched fart.

The thing on the bed stopped moving.

Doc closed the door soundlessly. The lock was nothing more than a metal hook and latch, and his fumbling fingers put it in place. Had it seen him? Had it *heard* him? He pressed his ear to the door.

Nothing. No footsteps, no creaking floorboards, no nails plunging into—

He tried not to think about it, instead glancing around the room for a potential escape route. But the small washroom, of course, had no way out. No windows, and no doors except the one he stood in front of. There was a small plughole, and an air conditioning vent coming from the ceiling, but it was too narrow for him to fit through. Too narrow for *anyone* to fit through.

And so he stood and waited, his heart threatening to leap from his chest and splat messily onto the floor.

The door handle turned. Sweat ran down Doc's forehead, down the back of his neck, his toes curling in dreadful anticipation. A nail rammed through the door, emerging an inch from his face. Tiny flakes of broken wood spat through the air, blood dripping from the point of the nail. Kelly's blood. He ran from the door, bumping up against the wall as the nail withdrew.

"Stay back," he said in a tremulous voice. "I've... I've got a gun."

A gun? He didn't even have a pair of pants, never mind a fucking gun. The only feasible weapon in sight was the metal bucket he had used when washing his genitals. It would have to do. As he crossed the room, the door burst open behind him. The floor was wet, and in his shock and surprise, his feet slid out from under him. Doc dropped to his knees, hearing them crack as he reached desperate fingers towards the bucket.

Something sharp pierced him below his shoulder blade. He yelped in agony, glancing down at the nail protruding absurdly from his flesh. Blood spattered onto the floor beneath him. The second nail entered below his clavicle, bursting out the other side. With a crazed lunge he threw himself forwards, the nails sliding excruciatingly through him... but not far enough. The creature raised its arms, and Doc slid back down. His feet left the floor, the creature carrying him towards the toilet bowl.

"Stop!" he cried. "Please, I've got money!"

Then the toilet was rushing towards his face, the slender figure slamming him down with inhuman ferocity. Doc's teeth cracked off the rim. The impact decimated the entire top row, white shards of shattered enamel decorating the contents of the bowl like frosting on a chocolate cake. The pain was immense, and Doc swooned in and out of consciousness. He forgot about the nails in his chest, for they were nothing compared to the unbearable throbbing in his ruined mouth, and when the creature shifted its arms, Doc's face hovered above his own piss and shit and blood.

"No," he tried to say, but what came out was a rattling exhalation. The creature thrust Doc forwards, plunging his face into his own feces. He closed his mouth, but it was too late, and he choked on the foul taste of excrement, before regurgitating it, the vomit mingling with his own shit in his mouth and preventing him from breathing.

He kicked, and he punched, but the creature pressed him down harder, the nails tearing through his skin, grinding against his bones. As Doc expelled a final flood of shit down his thighs, he opened his mouth one last time in an attempt to scream.

He was dead before he even had the chance.

**18**

———

The main entrance was in chaos.

Packed tightly into the hallway, the group of men lined up by the front door, taking turns barging into it. Candy knew it would do no good. She stood at the back, raising a cigarette to her dry lips as one man aimed several vicious kicks at the door.

"Keep trying," urged Martha.

"I have to get out of here," said the man Candy remembered as Mickey. His nasal voice made him sound like a gangster in a Jimmy Cagney movie. "I told my wife I'd be in all night. My kid's home alone. He's only four."

Foxy's regular, Hart, took a run at the door. Despite his imposing size, he bounced off it uselessly. He turned to Martha. "That chain's going nowhere. You got a gun? Maybe we can blow it off."

"We should call the cops," said Candy.

"Stay out of this," said Martha. She looked at Hart. "I've got a pocket pistol. It's not much."

Hart shook his head. "That won't do. We need a shotgun. Or a Magnum."

"This is a brothel, not a fucking armory," snapped Martha.

"We need to call the cops," said Candy. "A man's dead."

Hart whirled on her, the beads of sweat on his bald head glistening under the lights. "Nobody's calling the pigs. Not 'til I'm out of here."

"Damn right," said another man. "I ain't getting caught up in this. I've got a reputation."

"What the hell's going on?" said a new voice. Candy turned to see a bleary-eyed man coming down the stairs, tucking his shirt into his blue jeans. Foxy followed behind him. She nodded at Candy, confusion on her face.

"Those religious assholes out front have locked us in," said Hart.

"We need to call the cops," said Candy, louder this time.

"Would you shut the fuck up about the damn cops?" roared Hart. "I can't be arrested today. None of us can. How about you, little girl? Can you afford it?"

"A man's dead!" she shouted. "A man's dead, and all you care about is—"

One of the men — a middle-aged jerk with a red face and a tweed suit — slapped her. "Keep quiet!" he snapped, then turned back to the throng of testosterone by the door.

Shocked, Candy leaned against the wall.

"Leave her alone, asshole!" Foxy shouted at the man, as she ran down the remaining stairs and came to Candy's side. He didn't seem to hear her. Or perhaps he simply didn't care?

"We could try to reason with them," Mickey was saying, ignoring the simmering tension. "Maybe, y'know, if we ask nicely, and explain things, they'll let us out?"

While the men debated this intriguing possibility,

Candy looked at Foxy. "They killed Joseph," she said. "He's dead."

So much death in one night. So much violence and carnage. It didn't seem real. None of it did.

And as the men argued and sniped at each other, Martha barely keeping them in check, Candy thought about Joseph's corpse. Was it still outside in the alley? Would someone notice it? Or had it already been disposed of like she had done with the priest? She wondered if the girl he was going on a date with would think he had stood her up. It was silly, she knew, but she couldn't help it.

"Candy," said Foxy. "We gotta get outta here." She wore an expression of worry... or perhaps even fear? Whatever it was, Candy was unused to seeing the unflappable Foxy looking so concerned. "Upstairs," said Foxy, "I saw something."

Candy wiped the tears from her eyes, mascara staining the back of her hand in a black smear. "What was it?"

"I don't know. I don't know if it was real, or... *shit,* I don't know."

"What about Sandra? Have you—"

"I've not seen her since the doctor looked at you. Not since she—"

"Went to the basement," said Candy. The two girls locked eyes, and Candy gripped Foxy's hand. In a quiet voice, she said, "I'm gonna call the cops."

"You can't. Not right now. Those men will..."

"They'll what? Kill me?"

"Yeah," Foxy whispered. "Yeah, they might. Believe me, *nothing's* more dangerous than a group of angry white men."

"I guess you're right," said Candy. If she called the cops now, she didn't know *what* the men would do. They were frightened and backed into a corner. Like feral dogs, their only recourse would be to lash out with teeth bared. She glanced over at them. Their discussion had come to an end, and they were back to attempting to break down the door. Her thoughts returned to the figure she had seen walking up the stairs after Joseph's death. That strange, ghoulish man, so hunched and thin, like he was one hundred years old. Who *was* he?

Using Foxy for balance, Candy got to her feet and hobbled towards Martha. She tugged on the woman's chiffon sleeve.

"Shouldn't we get everyone together?"

Martha didn't look at her. "Why?"

"So we're all safe. Who's still upstairs?"

"Safe?" Martha turned to her, her face a mask of contempt. "Why wouldn't anyone upstairs be *safe?*"

Candy struggled to find the words. "It's just... I saw someone earlier. Someone who shouldn't be here."

"Make sense, girl."

Candy's fists clenched in frustration. "I mean... what if they've not just locked us inside? What if they've locked someone inside *with* us?"

Martha stared at her. The corner of her mouth crept into a sneer. "You know what? I've had enough of your shit tonight. You're fired. Clear out your locker, and don't come back."

"What?"

"I told you. You're finished. Go sell your dimpled ass on the street where you belong."

One of the men rammed into the door. The chain stretched taut with a sharp metallic chime.

"Martha, please," said Candy.

"Enough. This is all your fault, you realize that?"

More tears sprang to Candy's eyes, and she hated herself for it. "It's *not.*"

Martha moved closer, until her nose was practically touching Candy's. "You killed the priest. You couldn't have just fucked him like anyone else, could you?"

"He was going to—"

"Shut up, and get the fuck out of here. Once we get these doors open, I don't ever want to see you again, do you understand?"

"But—"

*"Do you understand?"*

Candy nodded. She stumbled towards Foxy, who wrapped her in a hug and let her cry onto her shoulder. She couldn't afford to lose her job. Oh, she knew it was ridiculous to worry about it at a time like this... but was it, really? This danger would pass. It was fleeting. They would get out, eventually, when someone called the cops. But living in New York with no money and no job? That was an even bigger issue. She had spent a year building up her client base, and now it was all gone.

Another man thudded into the door. The jolt made her flinch, and then the men were arguing again.

She tried to think. Perhaps if she could come up with a way out that didn't involve the cops, Martha would forgive her? Maybe she could get her job back. She didn't want to work the streets. They were dangerous. In here, the girls looked out for one another. They were colleagues, even friends. But on the streets — the domain of the weirdos — you were alone. If you went missing from there, no one noticed. No one cared.

"What about the roof?" she said.

Martha shook her head. "I've already considered that. How are we going to get four storeys down?"

"We…"

"We could tie bed sheets into a rope," said Foxy. "We could do that, and climb down."

Hart had been listening in. "One at a time? If those punks outside are as dangerous as she says, they'll pick us off one-by-one like sitting ducks. No, we need to get out together."

"Or be discreet," said Foxy's sleepy looking client. "Is there an underground passage? A basement or cellar?"

"There's a basement," said Martha, "But it doesn't lead anywhere."

"Well, you'd better think of something, bitch," said Hart. "And make it quick, 'cos I ain't spending the night here, no matter how many of these cunts you offer me as compensation."

Candy shivered. She wrapped her arms around herself, rubbing at her skin. God, it was freezing. Her eyes traveled up to the silver box that protruded from the ceiling, blasting cold air at her.

"What about the air ducts?" she asked.

"What about them?" laughed Martha dryly. "Who's going to fit through those? You?"

"I can try." She stood and stared at the vent. It was small. She figured she could fit her top half through no problem — her tits weren't big like Foxy or Daniella's — but she didn't think her ass would make it. And what if she came to a corner? Those old vents turned at sharp angles. No, it was a dumb idea. But she had to keep thinking.

Regardless of what Martha said, Candy knew their lives depended on it.

## 19

OFFICER COLT SETTLED INTO THE CRUISER AND SLAMMED THE door. He watched Maroney through the rain-streaked windshield, the man's pants coated in mud from where he had fallen into the open grave. Homicide were on the scene now, and the detectives had made it clear the two men's services were no longer required.

Maroney climbed in alongside him, water dripping from the tip of his nose.

"Fucking homicide," he said. "Gonna take all the credit."

Colt looked at himself in the rearview. He was getting old, his hairline receding fast. "You want to spend all night digging around in a graveyard in the rain? Be my guest. I'm getting a burger."

"You can eat after seeing that?"

"Sure. Might hold the ketchup, though."

Maroney didn't laugh. He stared forwards, wiping his hands on his thighs. "Hey, man. What the fuck *was* that?"

"What was *what*?"

"That tunnel. Shit... what do you think did that?"

"That's for homicide to figure out."

"It looked like..."

Colt waited for Maroney to finish the sentence. When the younger man didn't, he prompted him out of curiosity. "Looked like what?"

Maroney ran a hand through his thick black hair. It came away soaked, and Colt fought back a pang of jealousy. "It's gonna sound crazy," said the younger man, "but it looked like something dug its way *out* of there."

"So it's a zombie, right? Is that what you're telling me?"

Maroney shook his head. "I'm serious. The hole in the casket. The broken pieces were on top, like something had... I dunno, punched its way out. If someone had broken in — grave robbers or whatever — the pieces would be *inside.*"

"The tunnel was dug by an animal."

"Okay, sure, an animal. But that casket was empty. Where was the body?"

"Animal ate it."

"What animal?"

Colt shrugged. "The big corpse-eating kind. I don't know, you dumb shit. Do I look like a zookeeper to you?"

He turned the key, and the engine choked into life. Colt flicked the wipers on, watching as the homicide detectives cleared the area, cordoning it off and trying to look important. They had lifted the girl out of the grave, and now led her towards an ambulance parked outside the cemetery. The rain had washed most of the blood off her face, though Colt noted her panties still trailed from her ankle. She walked stiffly, like a—

*A zombie?*

Colt snorted. Maroney was young, he supposed. He had a lot to learn, but he would be a good cop one day, if he lived long enough. The streets were rough, and only getting rougher. The pimps, the pushers, the hookers, the junkies, the muggers, the killers, the rapists... every year, there were more of them. Despite all the mayor's fancy talk of *law and order,* little was done about it. The crooks outnumbered the cops two-to-one these days. Soon, they'd be running the city. In a few years, they'd be in charge of the whole damn country.

The paramedics were helping the girl into the rear of the ambulance.

*Poor thing,* he thought.

She came out here to fool around with her boyfriend, and instead watched his head get crushed by a tombstone. He wondered if she'd ever recover, ever forget it. It was possible to acclimatize to death, as Colt knew all too well. But it took a long time. And if it didn't, you were most likely a psychopath.

The ambulance doors closed and the paramedics jogged around to the front. Soon, the reverse lights came on, turning the rain into golden drops that hammered the sidewalk and gushed down the drains.

Colt put the cruiser in gear, waiting for the ambulance to leave first. It eased onto the road, heading towards the hospital, and Colt pulled out after it. They would follow for a while until they passed his favorite burger joint. He stole a glance at Maroney. The man's pale face glowed a sickly yellow in the street lights.

"Sure you're not hungry?" he asked with a grin.

"The fuck I am," said Maroney. He sniffed at his sleeve. "I *literally* smell like death."

"You fuck around in graves, that's gonna happen."

"I wasn't *fucking around.* The ground just... collapsed. One second I was standing there, and the next... honestly, man, I damn near shit my pants."

"Want me to write that in the report?"

Maroney chuckled. "I'd rather you—" his eyes widened "—Oh shit, *look out!*"

Colt had learned from years on the force to trust the intuition of his partners, and Maroney was no different. As an officer, he may have been wet around the ears, but that didn't prevent Colt from jerking his foot down on the brake without hesitation. He looked through the windshield in time to see the ambulance tilting forwards, its back wheels rising from the ground. The road seemed to hungrily devour it, the concrete crumbling and falling away as an enormous sinkhole opened up in the middle of the street. The vehicle rose until it was on the precipice of toppling completely over, hung there for several seconds... and then dropped into the gulf.

Colt's cruiser skidded, the wheels spinning on the wet surface, and came to a halt as the lights in the surrounding buildings flicked on, tired faces peering from windows to see what the commotion was.

"What the fuck," breathed Maroney, but Colt was already opening his door. He stepped out of the cruiser and looked on in horror. The road had split open, the chasm stretching as wide as both sidewalks, and running for at least fifty feet. Colt took a step closer to the edge and peered down at the ambulance, which lay on its roof about ten feet below him. Thank Christ they hadn't been above a subway station or line, or things could have been much worse.

"Shit," he said, as he noticed the widening cracks, hundreds of them racing from the trench. He took a couple of steps back and pounded his fist on the hood of the cruiser.

"Get out," he said to Maroney.

Curious onlookers and gawkers emerged from behind their doors.

"Everybody, stay back!"

The ground was giving way. He ran from the cracks, which seemed to reach for him like grasping, frenzied fingers, and pressed himself up against the wall of a laundromat. They carried on past him, and he watched as Maroney jogged to safety. The cruiser wobbled precariously, then toppled into the rapidly extending hole with a crash. Glass broke, the headlights angled upwards, lighting a window three floors above them.

The cracks continued, curving as if following some set path. They passed a lamppost and it toppled onto a parked sedan, shattering the windows and denting the roof. More concrete crumbled, until the channel stretched all the way back to the cemetery.

Car alarms blared, and in the opposite direction, a fire hydrant burst, shooting water high into the air. But Colt wasn't interested in that. He had spotted something else. Something deeply concerning.

"Fuck me," he said, taking tentative steps towards the vast channel that had ruptured the street like an axe wound. "It can't be." He turned away, racing back to the ambulance. Standing on the edge of the chasm, he crouched and looked in.

There, beneath the falling concrete and debris, he could see it. No, he could see *them*. Tunnels. Dozens of them, like the inside of a termite mound.

"Colt, don't!" he heard Maroney shout, but he ignored the man and hopped down into the channel. Already it was filling with rain. He turned back to Maroney. "Get them out of the ambulance," he shouted, then reverted his attention to the tunnels. He grabbed the flashlight from his pocket and shone the beam in.

Colt squinted. He thought he saw movement ahead. *Way* ahead, just out of reach of his flashlight beam.

He leaned in further. Dirt trickled onto the back of his neck, falling down his shirt. The tunnels were too unstable. He couldn't — no, he *wouldn't* — go any further. He stood, and started back towards the ambulance to assist Maroney. Behind him, he heard the tunnels collapse.

He didn't dare look back.

**20**

———

LINDA WAS TIRED.

She lay beneath the crumpled sheets, watching as her john dressed. He tugged a pair of corduroy pants over his muscular ass and stuffed his feet into worn sneakers, bending to tie the laces. He didn't say a word as he did so, and that was A-OK with Linda. The night's events had taken a toll on her. She had dealt with Vern, and then moved onto this guy, whose name she didn't remember. But throughout both sexual encounters, she had been unable to stop thinking about the dead priest, and Candy, covered in blood. It was an image she worried would never leave her. How must Candy be feeling right now? Had she managed to feign ecstasy with Joseph? She would have tried. Like any job in the service industry, Martha expected her employees to leave their baggage at the door. It didn't matter what was going on in your personal life — money problems, boyfriend issues, or murdering a priest — when you were with a client, you were to be polite, obedient, and courteous. And above all, make them come. She supposed that last point was where her job differed from that of a waitress or a salesperson.

Her client — Martha insisted the girls called them clients, not johns, though no one really paid attention to that — finished dressing. Without a look back, he strode towards the door.

"Hey, sugar," she cooed. "No tip for—"

The door slammed behind him.

"That motherfucker," said Linda. Nothing? *Nothing?* Okay, so she was off her game tonight, but she *had* witnessed a murder. She supposed her client — Roy, that was his name, she remembered now — couldn't have known, but still... no tip at all? Zero, zilch, nada? She had sucked his cock until it throbbed in her mouth, then ridden him until he was ready, at which point she had pulled away and let him come, as requested, on her tits... and she got *nothing* for it?

"Cheap bastard," she muttered, sliding out from under the covers and resting her feet on the cold wooden floor. Though she had washed the worst of his residue off her chest, a slight stickiness remained. She needed a proper shower downstairs. Or better yet, a bath. She hadn't had one of those in months. Her friend, a part-time model, had one in her apartment, and let Linda use it whenever she was out of town on assignment, on the condition that she watered her plants.

Linda stood and yawned and stretched, then rubbed her eyes and looked for her clothes. They were strewn around the room, and she gathered them and laid them on the bed. Something was missing.

Her panties.

They shouldn't be hard to find. They were bright red, with a black hand print over the seat. Not her sexiest underwear, but it was laundry day, and what's a poor hooker to do?

"Roy, you'd better not be a goddamn panty thief," she said as she scoured the room.

It was a common problem, especially with college kids. They always wanted a souvenir, something to show their friends, or to sniff as they jerked off in their parents' basement. One time, a guy had even asked to cut off some of her pubic hair so he could wear it in a locket. He was too creepy, and Linda had asked Martha to bar him from the premises. She only saw him again once, on the evening news; his mugshot after he had raped, killed, and dismembered a prostitute.

The memory made her shiver. Well, that, and the fact she was still naked and the room was fucking freezing. She got down on her hands and knees, searching for her missing underpants...

She smiled.

"Well, well, well," she grinned, as she reached under the bed. "What... do we have... here!"

Her fingers closed over a leather wallet. She pulled it out and perched on the bed. Inside were several tens and twenties. She removed one twenty and placed it next to her.

"That's for not leaving a tip."

Her grin widened, and she pulled out a ten.

"And that's for not saying thank you."

Her fingers grasped another note.

"You know what? I think I'll just keep it all."

There was a credit card tucked into one of the pockets, belonging to a Marvin Harrison. Behind it she found a small, passport sized photograph. Linda tugged it free. Roy — or Marvin, she supposed — smiled back at her. There was a woman with him, much older, with gray hair and a kind, wrinkled face. They looked similar.

"You carry a picture of your mom, Roy? That's pretty cute."

Damn, now she felt bad. She never should have looked at the photo. It had humanized him too much. He was no longer just a piece of meat to her, like she undoubtedly was to him. He was a man who loved his mother. Shit, was that a dog too? It was. A small, black-faced dog, with more wrinkles than the woman and a drooping tongue.

So he loved his mom *and* he had a dog?

Linda sighed. "Fine, I'll give you your fucking wallet back," she said. She tucked the ten in with the other bills, and picked up the twenty. "Actually, *you* can stay. I do deserve a tip, don't I?"

She climbed onto the bed and stared at the air vent set into the wall. With the headboard acting as a footrest, she lifted the metal grate and scrambled inside the vent up to her waist. The metal was unpleasantly chilly against her belly and breasts, and she gasped as her skin made contact. Reaching her arm out, she groped around the dusty air duct until she found it.

A small metal box.

Then she shuffled out of the vent and grabbed her shorts, plucking the key from them and opening the box.

She stuffed the twenty in, alongside more bills and coins and trinkets she had 'collected' from clients over the years, and stood on the headboard again. Cold air blasted her face from the open vent, billowing her hair. She shoved the box inside as far as it would go, metal scraping against metal with a piercing shriek.

The vent was her own personal safe. It was secure, because no one else could fit into it, and the chances of

Martha paying someone to come in and clean the vents were so small you would need a microscope to find them.

She closed the vent and quickly dressed in her shorts and mesh top. If she was quick, she could catch Roy before he left and give him his wallet back. Minus the twenty bucks, naturally.

She walked to the door and touched the handle. The metal was unusually cold, even for this place, and she recoiled. "Huh," she said, then pressed the handle down and stepped into the corridor.

"Hey Roy, you forgot..."

The wallet fell from her hand.

Roy lay on the floor, his back against the wall. A wide pool of blood surrounded him.

Linda took a single step forwards. Her knee buckled, and she shot a hand out for balance. Roy's legs were splayed, his guts spread out between them in a steaming heap of viscera. She could smell him, the foul stench of violent death. It couldn't be real, and yet it was. Her second dead body in the space of one night. Linda's mind reeled. Were the killings connected?

*Candy.*

She had killed the priest, there was no doubt about that. Had she murdered Roy, too? Was Candy a deranged, psychopathic killer? No, it was impossible. Candy was a nice girl, a quiet girl... but didn't they always say it was the quiet ones you had to watch?

*So do something!*

She had to stop standing there like a total idiot and go tell someone. Martha couldn't cover *this* one up. There was a maniac on the loose, prowling the corridors, and whether it was Candy or someone else, they had to be stopped. Come to think of it, where *was* the killer?

She listened, hearing nothing but competing radios playing a mixture of soul, pop, and hard rock, the discordant rhythms of Cheap Trick and Willie Hutch and Sheena Easton weaving an unnerving spell.

Despite the cold, Linda realized she was sweating.

What if the killer was watching her right now? And if so, were they in front of or behind her? Which staircase was safest? She considered shouting for help, but the killer had to be nearby, lurking in one of the rooms. But which one? She gazed down the corridor. The doors were all closed.

*"Help..."*

The voice startled her. It was Roy. The poor man was still alive, his chest rising with each labored breath. Linda put a finger to her lips. She didn't know what else to do. She couldn't save him. His intestines were...

*"Help!"* he said, louder this time.

*I'm sorry,* Linda mouthed at him. Tears ran down her cheeks. *I'm so sorry.*

Roy glared at her. His eyes rolled up, displaying the putrid whites, and he managed to raise one arm. *"She's here! She's here!"* he spluttered with his dying breath, and Linda thought she saw him smile.

She backed away, shaking her head. "Please," she whispered, and from somewhere nearby came an ungodly shriek. One of the wooden doors splintered out in a vicious explosion as a girl's head smashed through it. It was Beatrice, her hair disheveled, her face a grisly mess of scratches and puncture wounds. She turned to Linda and opened her mouth, crimson fluid dribbling down her chin.

"Run," she said, and then a hand appeared through the hole in the door, a hand with an enormous nail sticking through it. It grabbed the top of Beatrice's head, the nail sinking into her cranium, hot blood bubbling from her skull and gushing down her face.

Roy's arm dropped lifelessly to the floor, and Linda took it as her cue to run. Without thinking, she scurried back into the bedroom and slammed the door, closing the latch.

Roy was dead. Beatrice was dead. They were all dead. Who was still alive? Had the killer started downstairs and worked their way up? And that hand... that horrible, grotesque hand. It didn't belong to Candy, that was for sure. It reminded her of someone, or some*thing,* though she couldn't place it, not when her heart was beating this fast, and not when her mind was racing wildly in obscene panic.

She leaned back against the door, sobbing.

The handle rattled, and she screamed and stumbled backwards into the bedroom.

"Leave me alone," she said. "Please."

The door opened, hitting against the latch and coming to a stop. Linda looked around the room. There was no way out. No way except...

She ran for the bed, leaping onto it so fast that she almost bounced off the mattress and back onto the floor. She fumbled the vent open with clumsy, numb hands, and stepped on the headboard, reaching in and grabbing the metal box, hurling it onto the bed as the door vibrated under the insistent pounding. The latch wouldn't hold much longer.

Linda hoisted herself into the duct, her legs dangling. She kicked off the wall, toenails scratching against the faded floral wallpaper as she squeezed into the cramped area. She had never been this far inside before. Freezing air rushed past her, the joins in the metal panels scraping at her clothes, her skin. She was all the way in now, her arms extended before her. There wasn't enough room to move them back. The walls were as wide as her shoulders, and she had to shuffle her body like a worm to make any progress.

She heard the door swing open and smash off the wall, the metal latch clattering to the floor. Whoever it was, they were inside now.

Linda froze. Aware that the narrow duct would amplify even the slightest movement, she waited. It was pitch black, the walls narrower than they had ever seemed before. Fighting claustrophobia, and unable to look over her shoulder, she carefully maneuvred onto her back. That way, she was able to lift her head and look down over her body towards the vent. It was visible, light streaming in through the thin shafts of the loose panel. How long would she have to wait here? Her veins pulsed with fear. Ten minutes? An hour? All night? She didn't think she could take it. She raised her head further and it bumped off the top of the air duct. Should she move closer and try to listen?

A dark shape appeared at the vent.

Linda wanted to scream. A pressure built between her legs, a tightness in her bladder. Was the killer looking in at her? Could he *see* her?

Two beady red eyes set into the murky shadows of a face peered back at her, and her bladder finally released. She clamped her thighs together to prevent it, but it was useless. The urine trickled noisily onto the metal panel, and Linda knew she had no choice.

She had to move.

She turned clumsily onto her front again, shuffling further into the duct. Where would it take her? Behind, the vent creaked open. Surely they wouldn't be able to follow her? No fully grown adult could fit through. Linda had the body of a teenage boy — something which seemed to be a selling point for certain clients — but her lack of curves allowed her access to the duct. No one else could possibly—

But they *were* following. She heard metal grinding, as the nails in the killer's hands pierced through the panels, and only then did Linda recall where she had seen those hands before.

Had she not been in a desperate flight from a killer, she may have lost her mind at that point. But there was no time. The madness would come later, and she would welcome it with a smile and a sigh of weary resignation. For now, she had to keep going.

There was light ahead of her. Another vent. It would probably be sealed, but the building was seemingly held together with a lick and a prayer, so who knew? It might open. The vent in her room was only fixed in place by one rusted screw.

Her mesh top caught on a panel edge and tore. For a second, she thought it was her skin. She rolled, angling herself so that her shoulders pointed towards the corners, and looked back. All she could see was darkness. Then it was there, appearing from the obsidian emptiness, dragging itself along with the nails in its hands. Linda screamed. She dug her fingertips into the joins in the panels and hauled herself forwards until she reached the vent.

It wouldn't open.

She placed her hands on the metal grate and pushed, trying to gain as much leverage as the narrow tunnel would allow.

The crawling statue never stopped, never slowed. It kept coming for her. Linda had the feeling it would *never* give up. She looked through the vent. Maybe someone was in there?

"Help me!" she screamed. The words caught and died on her tongue.

She saw a person inside, on the bed. They had been torn apart. The sheets were stained the deepest, darkest red she had ever seen, and the mess that lay atop them resembled the unwashed floor of a slaughterhouse.

Driven by crazed, unimaginable fear, Linda kept moving. Her hair caught on something, but she didn't stop. She simply jerked her head to tear the strands from her scalp and crawled onwards. The duct seemed to narrow at parts, and she had to angle her body just right to slide through, cutting herself on the exposed screws that crudely attached the panels to each other. She came to another vent, and discovered it was also sealed.

What if they all were? How far could she go? It had to end somewhere, but with what? A filtration unit? A fan? She didn't know, but she refused to let the lack of knowledge slow her progress. Her hands found something ahead of her. A panel. A dead end? No, a corner. The duct turned left at a sharp right angle.

"Oh fuckfuckfuckfuckfuck," whimpered Linda. It would be tight. She tried to turn onto her side, but the roof was too low. She could barely move. Using her feet to propel her, she scraped along the panels towards the bend, the razor-edged metal peeling off a slice of her thigh like a cheese grater.

Her arms made it around okay, followed by her head. Her eyes widened. Ahead, through a lazily spinning fan, she saw lights. The city! It was the way out. All she needed to do was get past this bend.

Angling her body as best she could, Linda pushed against the panels with the soles of her feet. A sharp screw pierced the webbing of her big toe, but she no longer felt any pain. She felt nothing except the desire to survive.

Her body twisted as she attempted to round the corner. If only there was an inch more room. Hell, half an inch! She pushed, she pulled, her fingernails finding a panel edge and digging in.

Something touched her foot. A rat?

No. The figure from the crucifix.

Grasping fingertips brushed her flesh.

"Leave me alone!"

Pressing her soles against the side of the duct, she gave one final almighty push. The sharp corner sheared off more layers of skin on her belly, and though Linda screamed, she still made it around the bend.

She was free! Now all that stood between her and the outside was—

The tip of one of the spikes plunged into her ankle, pinning her to the metal like a butterfly. She tried to wrench her leg free, but it was no use.

She was stuck.

"No!" she cried, as the misshapen, warped head appeared, its lank hair streaming over thin wooden shoulders, and the eyes, those awful red eyes that pierced her soul, fixed on her.

As jets of blood spurted from her ankle, and the darkness seemed to close in, Linda clasped her hands together and started to pray.

It was all she could think to do.

**21**

———

Candy was slumped on the floor of the waiting room with her head in her hands when she heard the screams. They were oddly muted, like the sound from a TV with a busted aerial.

"You hear that?"

Foxy stopped pacing and looked at her distractedly. "Hear what?"

Candy stood, her joints aching as she did so. Her foot throbbed madly. It was badly swollen, with a dark purple bruise wrapped protectively around the skin. "I think it was Linda."

"I didn't hear anything," said Foxy, and she resumed pacing, muttering, "Didn't hear anything at all."

Candy studied her friend's face. "Foxy, what did you see up there?"

"Nothing, I already told you that."

"Come on. You're my best friend... maybe my only friend. You know you can tell me, right?"

"Yeah, I know. I'm okay, it's just... look, I'll be better once we get out of here, that's all."

"You sure? Because if you did see—"

"I didn't see a damn thing," said Foxy, and turned away as if that settled the matter.

In the reception area, the men squabbled noisily, their voices bleeding through the wall. They had given up on trying to open the door, and were now deciding whether or not to try shooting the chain off with Martha's pistol. Most agreed it would draw the attention of the cops, and the idea was promptly discarded. The only other solution seemed to be the roof. Hart, who had assumed the role of group leader with his imposing size and natural charisma, had apparently changed his tune, and now argued vociferously in favor of Candy's idea, as long as he carried the pistol.

A strange echoing shriek drifted ethereally from above. Candy once more turned her gaze to the ceiling. "There it was again. The screams. You hear them that time?"

"Yeah," said Foxy. "That time I did."

They looked up towards the big silver air duct, and Candy said, "It's coming from in there."

"You think it's Linda?"

"I don't know. She's the only one of us who might fit."

"But what the hell would she be *doing* in there?"

Words deserted Candy. She motioned for Foxy to close the door, eliminating the sound of the arguing men, and tilted her head, listening. She heard it again, a piercing scream that reverberated through the duct like some distant echo of cosmic terror.

"Linda?" shouted Candy. Her shaky voice came out as little more than a croak, so she tried again. *"Linda?"*

There was no response, save the whistle of the air through the dusty vent.

The door to the waiting room opened, and they turned

to find Daniella staring at them from beneath her thick mop of black hair. "Martha says shut up. The men are thinking."

"I don't give a shit about the men," said Foxy. "Linda's in the ducts. It sounds like she's in trouble."

"Don't be stupid," sneered the Italian girl. "Nobody could fit in there."

Foxy didn't acknowledge her, instead turning her attention back to the vent. "Linda, you up there?"

"We have to find her," said Candy.

"She could be anywhere. The sound carries through the whole building."

"You guys are dumb," said Daniella, though she made no move to leave.

Candy glanced at her. "What's happening out there?"

Daniella shrugged. "They're thinking of trying the roof."

"So, *my* idea."

"I don't remember you saying anything about it. I only remember you getting fired in front of everybody." Daniella smiled. "That was humiliating for you."

Candy ignored the jibe. "Would somebody just call the damn cops already? This has gone too far."

"We can deal with it ourselves," said a new voice.

Martha.

The woman strode confidently into the room, shoving Daniella aside like she wasn't even there. "And I don't want to hear another word about the cops. They're like you — *not welcome.*"

Foxy stepped forwards. "Come on, Martha. Think about this. Candy's a hard worker, and you know it."

"Don't speak to me like that, you crack-whore. If it wasn't for *me*, you'd still be plying your trade in the back row of the grindhouses."

"Hey, keep it down a second," said Candy. "There's somebody moving in the vent."

Neither Foxy nor Martha were listening.

"Crack-whore?" said Foxy. "You got something to say to me, you jumped-up old white bitch?"

"I do, actually. You can leave too. I've had enough of *both* of your bullshit. I'm trying to run a business here, and my employees are a bunch of crack-whore ingrates!"

Candy strained her neck towards the vent. What *was* that sound? If only everyone else would keep quiet...

Foxy rose to her full height, five-eleven in heels. She looked down her nose at Martha. "You don't scare me, cunt. I survived just fine long before I met you, and I'll do it again."

"Perfect," said Martha, clapping her hands together. "There's a bum nearby who might spare you a dime if you suck his crooked, maggot-ridden dick." She smiled wickedly. "But only if you swallow."

Foxy shoved the older woman backwards. Martha stumbled onto the couch, then glared at Foxy with fire in her eyes.

"You fucking bi—"

*"Would you two shut up for one goddam second!"* screamed Candy, as the door opened and the men filed in.

"What the hell is going on in here?" said Hart. "I thought you had this under control, Martha?" He looked at Candy as she stared into the vent. "What's this crazy bitch doing... hey, wait a minute. Listen to that. It sounds like—"

A river of blood erupted from the ducts, gushing through the vent like a high velocity shower. It knocked Candy onto her ass, drenching her, a flood of thick, dark blood splattering off her body, off the floor, spraying in a wide circle around the room. Candy turned onto her hands and knees, but the endless downpour battered her spine and forced her face down into the ever-widening pool of plasma. She tried to scream but choked instead, spluttering up a mouthful of the coppery liquid. Foxy ran to her, grabbing her hand and sliding her across the floor on her knees as more and more blood poured out.

Only then, free from the raging torrent of gore, did Candy find her voice.

And this time, she did manage to scream.

# PART III

RESURRECTION

**22**

———

"WHAT THE FUCK IS GOING ON?" ASKED OFFICER MARONEY. The younger man stood by Colt with his arms dangling limply by his sides, surveying the devastation.

Unable to fully process what he had witnessed, Colt simply shook his head.

The chasm had claimed several more vehicles, all of which lay on their side or on their roofs in the vast, street-wide gulley. Store alarms screeched, dozens of them, the noise overwhelming, while the jet of water from the askew fire hydrant streamed into the air.

Colt scanned the length of the channel. It started from just outside the cemetery walls and continued down the street as far as the deli on the corner. He peered back at the cemetery, noting the squint tombstones, and recalling the tunnels they had found in the graves. He tried *not* to think about the empty coffin, nor about what he had seen crawling through the tunnel by the ambulance.

A violent sound caught his attention. He was glad of the distraction, at least until he spotted the wide cracks climbing the deli wall. They moved astonishingly quickly, shattering bricks as if they were made from polystyrene, the windows exploding outwards in showers of glass that sparkled under the streetlamps like falling snowflakes.

The cracks continued their inexorable journey up the wall, and Colt knew the building was going to come down. A group of pedestrians loitered nearby, attracted by the noise and the sick promise of blood. A couple of the less bloodthirsty citizens had climbed down into the channel to drag the injured and the deceased from their cars.

"Get back!" Colt roared. They didn't hear him. He unholstered his pistol, fumbling with it for too long, then fired into the air. "Get back! It's gonna—"

He was too late.

The wall peeled from the building, the onlookers too awestruck by the realization of their own mortality to move. A couple of folk did run, but no one stood a chance. The wall crashed down on top of them as Colt gazed slack-jawed at the interior of the deli and the apartments above it, the insides exposed like a corpse undergoing an autopsy. He saw the people inside scrambling for their lives as their floors buckled, but seconds later the rest of the building fell, taking the residents with it.

"Call it in!" Colt barked at Maroney. The man's indecision was writ large on his face. "Call it in, dammit!"

Another building started to crumble, this one on the other side of the street. It followed the line of the tunnels perfectly.

"Good God," said Colt, his feet frozen to the sidewalk.

The apartment block came crashing down. One second it was there, the next it was a pile of rubble. Though the thick clouds of dust spewed forth from the buildings obscured Colt's vision, he could hear the screams, wails, and moans coming from all around in a maddening aural phantasmagoria.

Men and women cried out in agony. Dogs barked. Thunder rumbled. Or was it another falling building?

"Colt! Hey, snap out of it!"

He realized his partner was shaking him.

"Colt, man, what are we gonna do?"

Colt stared at the man, trying to think of something to do, something to say. People were dying. All around him, people were *dying*. They needed help, and they would *get* help. Soon.

But not from him.

He was too busy, his brain firing into overdrive. He could offer assistance to those who currently required it, but then *more* people would die. Many more.

He was sure of it.

"Colt? Do you hear me?" asked Maroney, and Colt detected panic in his voice. That would do no good. An officer couldn't afford to panic. He had to keep a cool head at all times, and cast aside useless emotions. Lives depended on it.

He looked beyond Maroney and pointed in the direction of the channel. He understood now. Or, at least, he thought he did.

"They're going that way."

"Who is? We gotta help these—"

"It's a straight line. Don't you see?" He punched his fist into his palm. "It's a goddam *straight line*. We gotta follow it. Take the parallel street and drive alongside."

"What the *fuck* are you talking about?"

"Get in the cruiser," growled Colt. He didn't like to be sworn at.

"The cruiser? The cruiser's upside-fucking-down!"

"Then get me a civilian vehicle!"

Maroney nodded, uncomprehending. He hesitated. "You still want me to call it in to the station?"

"No time," said Colt, as he tucked his pistol back into its holster. And as Maroney headed off towards the nearest vehicle with a civilian behind the wheel, he quietly added, "They wouldn't fucking believe me anyway."

**23**

---

Candy was dimly aware of what was going on around her. She stared at the blood on her hands and screamed, unable to stop.

"Somebody shut her up!" yelled one of the men.

Blood dripped steadily from the vent, splashing into the scarlet puddle with monotonous regularity.

"You okay?" asked Foxy. "Candy, can you hear me?"

Everything was red. Foxy's face, the room... it was all *red*. Candy blinked and tried to wipe the crimson film from her eyes. It only made things worse. She was covered in blood. Soaked in it. Linda's blood.

"What happened?" someone shouted.

"Is that blood?" asked another.

That made Candy laugh. What did he *think* it was? Tomato soup? These men were the same in real life as they were in the bedroom.

No imagination.

"Don't worry," said Martha, though she didn't sound like she meant it. She stood together with the men, peering up in uncomprehending shock at the vent.

"Those goddam religious freaks." said Hart. "They must be inside the building. They've come to kill us." He turned to Martha. "Get the gun."

She didn't move. Hart took a handful of her gown and pulled her close. "I said get the fucking gun, *now!*"

"It's going to be okay," she said as she backed out of the room. "Everything is going to be fine."

Hart turned his attention to Candy. "What's going on?"

"Leave her alone," said Foxy.

"Fuck off. She knows something." He crouched before Candy and took her by the shoulders. "Bitch, listen to me! How many of them are there?"

Candy stared at him. "We need to call the cops," she said quietly.

"We ain't calling no goddam cops!"

"Can't you see she's in shock?" snapped Foxy. "Get off her!"

She grabbed Hart's arm, and he shoved her, sending her skidding across the blood-soaked floor.

"I don't listen to someone I pay to fuck up the ass," he roared, then turned back to Candy. "I asked you a question. How many of them are there?"

"F-four," she said. "No, five."

"Make up your mind!"

"I saw five. But there are more of them."

"It's that fucking priest," said Mickey as he lit a cigarette. "He's behind this."

"It can't be," said Candy. "He's—"

"I brought the gun," said Martha. She glared at Candy to shut her up, and held out the pistol. Hart took it, his huge hand making the weapon look like a toy.

"Okay," he said. "I'm through messing around. We stick

together and head to the roof. They can't surprise us up there. We'll make a rope out of bed sheets, and climb down one at a time. And if anyone tries to stop us…" He held the pistol out, closing one eye and aiming at an imaginary foe. A sly grin spread across his features. "I'll blow the motherfucker away."

The men murmured in agreement. Hart had asserted his authority as the alpha male, and the others cowed before him. If it hadn't been obvious before, now he had both a gun *and* a plan.

*My plan,* thought Candy, though she said nothing. She had a different plan now, one she wasn't going to tell anyone, not even Foxy. Not until the time was right. The mist of horror that had fogged her brain was dissolving. It was up to her now. She was the only one making any sense, the only one who truly understood the danger.

"I'll get the sheets," she said, her heart beating fast. "Me and Foxy."

Foxy looked at her like she thought she was insane. "We'll do *what?*"

"Good idea," grunted Hart. "Grab the sheets, then we'll tie them into a rope and head on up." He cradled the gun as he spoke, eyeing it reverentially. "Need any protection?"

"No," Candy said quickly. "The linens are the next door along. We'll be okay."

"I don't know—" Foxy started to say, before Candy cut her off with a glance.

They made their way across the room using each other for balance, their feet sliding on the blood like children playing in their socks on a newly waxed floor.

"What the hell are you doing?" whispered Foxy.

Candy didn't answer. She noticed Martha staring at her

with narrowed eyes, as if aware that some nefarious scheme was afoot. Candy ignored her. When she slipped and fell, no one laughed. They were too busy worrying about themselves, wrapped up in their own internal dramas. How would they explain this to their wives, their bosses? The lateness, the blood stains on their clothes, the haunted looks in their eyes?

Foxy helped her to her feet, and together they left the room, closing the door behind them. It was a relief to be free from the accusatory stares of the men, and the constant threat of violence that accompanied them. In the dim light of the corridor, Candy took Foxy's hand and started towards the reception area, beyond which lay Martha's office.

"What are you doing?" asked Foxy.

"Calling the cops."

Foxy yanked on her hand, stopping her. "You can't do that. You heard Hart... they'll kill you."

Candy pulled free from Foxy's grasp. "Seems everyone wants to kill me today. I'm getting used to it."

"Come on, *think* about this. You're acting crazy. If we stick with the men, we can get to the roof and climb down. Then we'll be safe."

"And what about Linda? Or Joseph? We just forget about them, huh? Sweep them under the carpet? Don't their families deserve to know what happened to them?"

"But what the fuck *did* happen to them?" Foxy was close enough for Candy to feel her breath on her face. She lowered her voice, quivering as if on the verge of tears. "Candy, upstairs, I... I saw something. Some*one*. And then I had a—"

"We don't have time for this. We have to call the cops. It's our only chance."

She wanted to listen to Foxy, she really did. But one of

the men could appear at any moment to check on them. And anyway, she had a pretty good idea of what the girl had witnessed. She had seen it too, hadn't she? Climbing the stairs.

The thing from the basement.

She turned and walked towards Martha's office, Foxy following in silence. Taking a wide berth around the staircase, the pair reached the reception area, passing a side door that led into a booth where Martha or a welcome girl would usually sit. The chair was empty, and a paperback with a yellow cover lay open on the desk, its spine cracked. The title was in Italian. Candy figured it must be Daniella's.

A single door lay behind the desk, and taped to it was a hand-written sign.

KNOCK OR FUCK OFF, it read.

Martha's office.

Candy reached for the handle, praying it wasn't locked.

*Thunk.*

A noise from behind. A door closing? Candy spun and looked past Foxy at the long expanse of corridor. "You hear that?"

"Yeah," whispered Foxy, though she kept her eyes facing forward. "Keep going."

Candy pushed the door open and entered Martha's office. It was dark.

*Of course it fucking is.*

She felt along the wall for the switch. Her fingers found it, and she hesitated.

*What if he's there? The man from the basement?*

She flicked the switch. The light came on, bathing the small room in a warm amber glow. No one lurched out of the shadows at her, no torrid nightmare men reaching for her with grasping talons. There was simply a desk and a chair and some sheets of paper, and there, over on the corner of the desk, was a phone. She picked up the receiver.

"Candy, someone's coming," said Foxy.

Sweat broke out on Candy's brow. She looked at her friend, then hooked her finger into the dial. Foxy moved to close the door. As she did so, it opened.

"There, I told you!" shrieked Daniella. "She's calling the police!"

There was a bustle of activity in the corridor

The men were coming.

Candy dialed the last digit and held the phone to her ear, waiting for someone to pick up.

*"9-1-1, what's your emergency?"*

"Help, send the cops to—"

Hart stormed in first. He snatched the phone from Candy's hand and slammed it onto the desk. The end of the receiver shattered. Candy screamed and threw herself backwards, but there was nowhere to go. She smacked into the wall, watching helplessly as Hart tore the line from the socket and brandished the broken receiver like a thug in a barroom brawl.

"You fucking cunt, you trying to frame me? Huh?" Spittle flew from his lips. "You calling the cops on me? I can't go to jail again, bitch!" He punctuated his words by smacking the receiver off the desk until it crumbled in his enormous hands.

"I'm sorry," Candy gasped. "But—"

He yanked her from the room by her arms, past the other men, past Martha, and past Daniella and her self-satisfied little smirk.

"Leave her alone!" cried Foxy.

Hart ignored her. He dragged Candy into the corridor, his fingertips sinking into her forearms, and threw her to the ground. She hit it, *hard,* and scrambled onto her hands and knees, ready to defend herself. Her gaze fell on the gun tucked into the waistband of his pants. He noticed her looking at it.

"Yeah, that's right. I oughta kill you." Judging by his furious expression, he seemed to be considering it.

"Please," said Candy. "I'm sorry."

He pulled the gun from his pants and pointed it at her, the stubby barrel inches from her face. "I oughta shoot you in the fucking head!"

"C'mon, man," said Mickey. "Let's get out of here while our hands are still clean."

"No," said Daniella. "Shoot her!"

"What?" shouted Candy.

Daniella shrugged. "Nothing personal."

Hart's huge finger closed over the trigger, his eyes narrowing as he glared at the sorry sight of Candy cowering on the floor, coated from head-to-toe in Linda's blood. No one moved. No one dared.

"Shit," said Hart, taking a deep breath and lowering the gun to his side. "Get her out of my sight."

Candy closed her eyes, remaining on the floor. The strength had left her limbs, and she felt like a discarded rag doll. Would Hart have shot her? In the heat of the moment, he might have done.

"You got somewhere we can put her?" Hart asked Martha. "I can't have this bitch getting in my way again, because next time, I *will* kill her. I fucking mean it."

Candy was only half-listening. She couldn't get up, her legs numb, her head still spinning. That had been too close. Too close, too close, too fucking close.

"Yeah, I got somewhere," answered Martha. She glanced past them all, down the corridor, her eyes settling on—

"No..." whispered Candy, for she knew what Martha was going to say.

The older woman raised her finger and pointed.

"The basement," she said. "We can lock her in the basement."

**24**

---



The basement.

God, the fucking *basement*.

She couldn't go back there. Not again. *Never* again.

Candy stumbled to her feet, adrenaline flooding her veins. She had to run. Where to? She didn't know. She couldn't think straight. All she knew was that if they put her in the basement, then this time she wasn't coming out.

She turned on her heels, but Hart was too fast, too strong. His burly arms wrapped around her, lifting her off the ground.

"In there," said Martha, pointing to the metal door. "I've got the key."

"No!" screamed Candy. "No, no, *no!*" She thrashed her legs, kicking Hart's thighs, aiming for his groin. "Not in there!"

But Hart didn't care. Nobody did. The big man held her effortlessly, his large strides carrying them down the corridor in seconds. The doorway loomed before them, chilling in its stark blackness, the door open and waiting.

"Please, not in there! I'll do anything! Please! I don't want to go in the basement!"

"Shoulda thought of that," grunted Hart, "before you called the—"

He suddenly jolted, spinning around, Candy's legs swinging out like a helpless baby.

"What the fuck?" said Hart. "Get this bitch off me!"

Candy tried to turn, desperate to see what was happening. She caught fleeting glimpses of Foxy's hands, the girl's fingers digging into Hart's face, hooking into his lips, his nostrils. Hart — still clutching Candy in a bearhug — ran backwards into the wall.

Foxy gasped in pain, then snarled, "Put... her... down."

Footsteps echoed down the corridor.

The other men were on their way.

"Get her!" cried Hart, his words slurred due to the attack. Then it was Foxy's turn to scream as the men caught up to her, dragging her off Hart and depositing her roughly on the ground. Candy heard her body smack off the floor, and craned her neck to see the men forming a circle around the fallen girl. Foxy tried to stand, but they lashed out with fierce kicks and punches, pummeling her, forcing her to curl into a ball, covering her head and face, as they rained down more blows.

"Stop!" screamed Candy. "You'll kill her!"

She squirmed wildly, fighting to free herself from Hart's vice-like grasp, desperate to protect her friend.

Then Hart tossed her unceremoniously forwards, through the doorway and into the uninviting darkness of the basement. She hurtled through the air, landing awkwardly on her broken foot and crumpling to the top of the wooden stairs. There was just enough time for her to spin and crawl towards the door, one arm outstretched, before it slammed shut with a deafening *clang*.

"No!" she roared. *"No!"*

She heard motion outside, the men still beating Foxy. Hammering her fists off the door, she cried out, begging, pleading, her sanity ebbing away. Metal rattled against metal as Martha inserted the key, and Candy listened as the deadbolt slotted into place.

"Let me out!"

Her voice was raw, tears streaming down her face.

*"We'll send someone back for you,"* came Martha's muted reply. *"Once we're out."*

Candy's fists ached, so she slapped her open palms against the door. The sounds on the other side died away, until Candy heard nothing but the useless smack of her own bloodstained hands against the door, and the ceaseless thudding of her heart.

Her hands slid down the metal, and she rested her forehead against it.

"Foxy?" she called out. "Are you there?"

No answer.

"Foxy?"

Was she dead? Had they killed her?

Of course not. They couldn't do that. After all, Martha had said she would send someone to rescue her, to let her out of the—

Candy broke down. It was a lie, wasn't it? Nobody was coming to rescue her. Absolutely nobody. She was trapped in here, and Foxy was dead, and she was all alone.

*Alone.*

In the basement.

She turned her head, gazing into the void, waiting for her eyes to adjust.

They didn't. She saw nothing but impenetrable darkness. Even when she held her own hand up to her face, she could make out no shape. It was as if she had lost her sight completely. She forced herself to stand on legs that threatened to crumble, running her hands across the door in search of the handle. She found it, and, though she knew it was useless, tried it anyway.

The door was locked.

She listened for that infernal scratching, for those dreadful footsteps...

All was quiet.

She slid her foot along the floor until she reached the edge of the first step. At least this way, she had her bearings.

*You've been down there already today. Nothing happened.*

But something *had* happened.

*You're still alive, though.*

That was true. Maybe whatever was down there couldn't hurt her? It could frighten her, sure. Scare the shit out of her, make her faint and bump her head. But so what? She had survived two encounters in this basement now. Two. What difference would a third time make? She would be ready. Prepared.

"Oh god," she whispered, her body breaking out in gooseflesh as a serpentine shiver slivered beneath her skin.

No, she was kidding herself. She couldn't do it, couldn't go down those stairs. No fucking way. She would wait here forever if she had to. And if she died of thirst, or exhaustion, or simply lost her damn mind, then that was infinitely preferable to whatever awaited down—

And that was when she heard the voice.

*"Candy?"*

She clenched her fists so hard, her nails dug into her palms, drawing blood.

*"Candy?"*

Again, more insistent this time. It was a voice she knew. A plaintive, broken voice she immediately recognized as Sandra's.

*"Candy, is that you?"*

"Sandra?"

*"Help me, Candy. Please. It's so dark down here."*

It couldn't be Sandra. It was impossible. Or was it? Martha had sent the girl down to the basement, and no one had seen her since. It made perfect sense for her to still be there.

*Perfect* sense.

"I'm up here," said Candy cautiously. "At the top of the stairs."

A moment's silence.

*"I can't move. Something attacked me. I'm hurt."*

"Can you make it up the stairs?"

*"I don't think so. Please, Candy... help me."*

Candy swallowed.

"I... I can't."

A long pause. Too long.

"Sandra? Are you there?"

*"I don't want to die down here, Candy. Don't leave me to die."*

What if it really *was* her? She couldn't leave Sandra on her own to perish in a whorehouse basement. She *had* to help her. It was her only option. A girl was *dying*... and all she had to do was walk down ten lousy steps to get to her. It would be better if the two of them were together in the darkness. Less frightening. And anyway, what the hell else was she gonna do? Wait up here by the door until she dropped dead herself?

Candy inched her good foot out towards the step again. Her toes curled around the edge.

"Okay, Sandra. I'm... I'm coming down."

Her fingers searched for the rail, found it, gripped it. Her entire body shook, violent tremors vibrating her limbs as tears of sheer terror rolled down her cheeks.

She held her foot out in midair, then placed it down on the first step.

"One," she said.

## 25

A DULL ACHE THROBBED IN FOXY'S TEMPLES AS HER EYES flickered open. She tried to stand, pain wracking her body. Giving up on standing, she rolled onto her back and stared at the ceiling.

The last thing she remembered was clinging on to Hart, scratching and beating him. After a while, it all came back to her. The other men rallying around their leader and pulling her to the floor. Kicking her, over and over, until she mercifully blacked out.

She shuffled towards the wall, her limbs in agony, and looked herself over. Bruises were forming over her bare arms and legs. They hadn't just beaten her. They had *trampled* her. Dirty bootprints covered her clothes from where they had stamped on her like a sick animal. Cuts and nicks marred her flesh, thin trickles of blood oozing from the small wounds.

How long had she been out? Where was everyone? Where was...

"Candy?"

The basement door was shut tight. Though every nerve

ending screamed for her not to, Foxy stood. She leaned against the wall until she felt able to walk, then staggered to the door and rattled the handle.

"Candy? You in there?"

Nothing.

"Candy? *Candy?*"

She thumped her fist against the metal.

No response.

The building was dreadfully quiet. All Foxy heard were the faint strains of a radio playing upstairs. Where were the men? And Martha and Daniella? Had they made it to the roof? Had they somehow escaped?

The corridor stretched into darkness. She was alone, and in terrible pain. Painkillers, that was what she needed. Something to take the edge off. She faced the reception area and started walking. As she passed the waiting room, she glanced in, wishing she hadn't when her eyes fell upon the liquid remains of Linda. Blood still dripped from the air conditioning unit, and Foxy feared she might pass out again. Instead, she carried on, heading towards the shower room. It, too, was quiet. *Dead* quiet. She slipped through the beaded curtain and entered the deserted area.

Jesus Christ, what was going on? A thought struck her. What if she was the last remaining person, and the killer — whoever it was — had found her in the corridor and left her for dead? Should she just head back there and lie down again? No, she couldn't do that. She had to at least *try* to find other survivors. Wincing in discomfort, she plodded towards the jackets hanging from the rail. Someone had to have painkillers with them. Screwing all night was no picnic for the female body.

She searched each pocket, coming away with tissues, sticks of gum, candy wrappers, handwritten notes...

"Come on," she breathed, her hands trembling. Did no one have... then Foxy broke into a smile. Her fingers brushed something, and she retrieved it from the pocket. A small, folded sheet of paper. She took it to the makeup desk and carefully unfolded the sheet, revealing a light dusting of white powder. There looked to be a couple of grams of coke in there. Sure, it wasn't exactly Tylenol, but it would numb the pain, and give her the boost she needed to continue. With nothing to cut or snort it with, she held the paper to her nose and inhaled. When she looked up at herself in the mirror, her nose was comically pale against her skin. She wiped the residue off and smeared it across her gums, then sat, waiting for the powder to work its magic.

As she did so, she wondered who else might still be alive. Martha and Danielle, possibly. Then there was Hart, who, if things had gone to plan, she would have been fucking right now. The four men who had beaten her, one of whom was Stephen, the john she had spent the previous hour with. Those seven could be around somewhere. But what about Beatrice and Paula, or Kelly? Hadn't they all been with clients when the shit went down? Could *they* still be alive? God, she hoped so.

She didn't want to be alone.

The drugs worked their way through her system, and soon she felt strong enough to stand. It was good shit, she thought, as her pain faded.

Feeling better — *much* better — the first thing she did was check the front doors. They were still chained shut. She peered out, gazing onto the quiet street. Alarms blared in the distance, and a light rain was falling. She briefly entertained the notion of squeezing through the gap, but doubted even Linda's slender frame would have been able to fit.

And so Foxy found herself standing at the foot of the

stairs, clenching and unclenching her fists. She stared up, wondering what she would find. Hopefully, some of the other girls were on level two. And if not, she would head for the roof herself. She wouldn't find anything on levels three and four. As far as she was aware, those floors hadn't been touched since the building's construction all those years ago.

Foxy took one last look over her shoulder, steeled herself, and started up the stairs.

## 26

Colt missed the familiar comforts of his police cruiser.

He couldn't seem to get the seat in the Mustang they had 'borrowed' to adjust to his frame, so he sat hunched up, his knees scraping the steering wheel.

That, however, was the least of his worries.

As he guided the vehicle through the rain-slicked streets, keeping one block between himself and the collapsing road, he encountered more and more devastation.

Cars and trucks jutted out of the treacherous channel like strange fauna. Sides of buildings had toppled, while fires blazed from inside the damaged structures. In the worst cases, whole blocks had crumbled to the ground. Ambulances and more cop cars roared past him on their way to the epicenter.

"Everyone's going the other direction," said Maroney, the passing vehicles' headlamps creating a strobing effect on his confused face. "Shouldn't we be following them?"

"They're going the wrong way."

Maroney nodded, unconvinced. "But half the cops in the city are—"

"*Going the wrong way.* We gotta *follow* this thing. It doesn't matter where it started. It matters where it's going." He paused. "Where *they're* going."

"Who're they? What are you talking about? It's an earthquake, man. It's not *going* anywhere. It's just happening."

Colt gripped the wheel, swerving onto the sidewalk to avoid an oncoming vehicle. He wanted to explain his reasoning to Maroney, but he couldn't bring himself to. It was too wild, too insane.

What he had seen in that tunnel... those people... those *things*...

He knew where they were heading. The gravedigger had told them, plain as day.

They were traveling back to where they had once resided.

They were tunneling towards the old Manhattan Riverfront Church.

Colt shuddered.

They were going *home*.

**27**

———

Candy hovered indecisively in the darkness.

She slid her foot along the step until her toes found the edge, then stepped down. The wood creaked beneath her weight.

"Two," she said, the sound of her voice reassuring amid the black oblivion.

*"Hurry, Candy. It's so dark."*

"I'm trying, Sandra. Keep talking."

Something brushed across her face, and she screamed, fighting the urge to run back up the stairs. It was a cobweb, nothing more. Spiders she could deal with. Same with vermin. She lived in New York City, for Christ's sake. It was the other things that lurked in the darkness that frightened her. Like that man she—

*Don't think about it.*

She inched her foot forwards, placing it on the next step. "Three."

Was that the glow of the furnace she could see? She squinted into the emptiness. Perhaps... and perhaps not.

Would the priest still be in there, or would his bones have turned to ash by now?

*Stop spooking yourself.*

Linda's blood had dried on her skin, and now cracked as she walked, a soft sound like a small animal's bones breaking.

*Would you stop?*

She couldn't help herself.

"Fuck it," she said, and quickly took several steps.

"Four... five."

At the fifth step, she froze, her blood running cold. Halfway there. Halfway down. The worst was over. Wasn't it?

"Sandra?"

No answer.

"Sandra? Are you still there?"

Of course she was. Where could she possibly have gone? Or perhaps she was dead. Candy had taken too long to perform the basic task of walking down a short flight of stairs, and now Sandra was—

*"They... hurt me..."*

Candy breathed a rattling sigh of relief.

"I'm coming. Almost there."

She took another step. "Six," she said, in a false display of bravado. "I'm on step six."

She could practically jump the rest of them, get it over with in one move. But the bones in her broken foot crunched with each step, and to jump now — into total uncertainty — could render her completely unable to walk. What use would she be then?

Having successfully argued herself out of jumping, she took the following step.

"Seven."

Something groaned behind her. She turned and looked,

seeing nothing through the inky darkness that threatened to overwhelm her. Why hadn't her eyes adjusted? God, she wished she had her lighter on her, but it was back in the locker room. What she wouldn't give for even the briefest illumination! But what if she *did* have her lighter, and she flicked the wheel and came face-to-face with that man she had seen, that shapeless atrocity, that abominable creature from within the old church, leering at her, lunging out of the shadows, reaching for—

"Eight," she said, forcing her way down.

God, so close!

She burst into tears.

"Come on," she whispered.

Two more remained. That was easy. Hell, she lived on the fifth floor of an apartment block. Over a hundred steps every day just to go outside. She could do this. Two steps. That was nothing. A *baby* could crawl down them. Fuck, she wanted a drink. More than anything, she wanted a drink. And a smoke. A smoke would be great. She wanted to go out with Sandra for that drink they had spoken about, and that one drink would turn into several, and maybe they would head back to Sandra's place a little tipsy, and share a joint, get high. She imagined offering to pose for that painting, stripping off in front of Sandra, watching her eyes widen, her cheeks redden, the two of them laughing about it, Sandra coming over to help her, getting close, close enough to smell her perfume, and then they would kiss, gentle at first, testing the waters, seeing if—

Another creak from behind.

"Is someone up there?" she asked.

For one delicious moment, she had lost herself in a fantasy, and it had felt good. To forget where she was, and why she was here, was wonderful, and all too fleeting. But now she was back. Back on the stairs, back in the basement.

"Nine." She took the penultimate step too fast, hurting her foot and almost overbalancing. She gripped the rail. Would falling have been so bad? It might have been the only way to cross the imaginary threshold.

"Nearly there," she called to the girl.

*"You can do it."*

She wondered if Foxy was okay. Should she go and check? Maybe the basement door was unlocked now. No, fuck that. She knew what her subconscious was doing. It was looking for excuses to flee.

*"One more step. Please... hurry."*

This was it. The last step. Afterwards, both her feet would be firmly planted on the hard, packed dirt of the basement floor. One more step. One more. Just one. Not three, not two... but one.

An involuntary whimper escaped Candy's lips, and though it made no difference, she closed her eyes.

She took the final step.

"Ten," she said, as her foot touched the ground. She waited for something dreadful to happen. When it didn't, she said, "I made it!"

There was no reply from Sandra.

Candy opened her eyes, expecting to see the light from the furnace. She heard it rumbling away, the snaps and hisses and cracks of burning embers sparking against the metal interior... but still she saw nothing.

"I'm coming," she called. She raised her injured foot and placed it in front of her, except nothing was there. No floor, no ground. Surprised, she almost toppled, gripping the rail as her foot landed on something hard again. Another step?

Had she miscounted? Back when she had quickly taken two, she must have—

*"Eleven,"* said Sandra.

*No, no, no...*

It wasn't right. She held her foot out, searching for the floor that had to be there. It dropped to another step.

*"Twelve."*

Sandra started to laugh, though it no longer sounded like her.

Candy kept going, step after step, panic veiling her mind.

*"Thirteen... fourteen... fifteen..."*

"No!" screamed Candy, unaware she was doing so. "No!"

Down she went, down and down and down the impossible staircase, as Sandra's manic laughter rang in her ears, and the walls of sanity began to crumble around her.

**28**

———

Foxy needed a weapon.

As she climbed the stairs, she tried to think of where she could locate one in the windowless whorehouse. There were no more guns she was aware of, nor any fire axes. There *was* a disused kitchen area downstairs, but she knew from experience that the drawers were bare.

She slowed as she neared the top of the first flight, peering down the second level corridor at the business floor, as Martha referred to it. The two levels above were empty, so this was her last chance to find something to defend herself with.

The first thing she spotted was a grotesquely mutilated corpse a few doors down. It was a man, his face butchered, guts splayed across the floor. Who the hell was *doing* this? The protestors? They were a bunch of middle class soccer moms and buttoned-up religious assholes. Brutal murder wasn't exactly their forte, unless they had hired someone to do it? A hitman, or the mob?

Out of curiosity, Foxy crept towards the first door,

nudging it open. The room was empty, the bedsheets stripped. The men must have taken them. It looked like they were going ahead with their plan of tying the sheets together and climbing down. The idea didn't thrill her — Foxy was not a fan of heights — but she would do literally anything right now to get out of this damn place. Hell, she'd take her chances and jump from the roof if it came to it.

The only point of interest in the room was the closet in the corner. Keeping low, she crept stealthily towards it. Her whole body felt numb, her head buzzing. Shit, that was some good coke!

Kneeling by the closet, she opened the door and looked inside. Handcuffs, a couple of vibrators, some masks... nothing useful for defending herself against a crazed killer. The metal candlestick holder by the side of the bed caught her eye, and she made her way over. It was nice and heavy, with a solid base. Good for cracking skulls? She hoped so. The candle was still lit, and she cupped her hand over the flame to keep it that way. She had no idea if the lights worked on next two levels.

Slowly, she exited the room and crept back to the stairs. She had never been on the roof before. None of the girls had. Why would they need to? A dark thought tormented her. What if there was no access? The whole building was a grim testament to shoddy workmanship. If the builders had neglected to include windows, what were the chances there was no way onto the roof?

She supposed she would find out soon enough. Though the fact she couldn't hear Martha and the men suggested they were up there already, perhaps even making their escape.

*Or they're dead.*

True. That was always a possibility.

She gazed up towards the next level, where the staircase vanished into darkness. Carefully, so as not to snuff the candle, she started up the stairs. The cocaine fired through her veins like a shot of pure adrenaline, urging her to speed up, but she knew she had to resist. Drugs were excellent painkillers, but not reliable for clear-headed decision making.

It was stiflingly hot, getting worse the higher she climbed, as if the air con hadn't been installed here. She wondered what time it was. With its lack of natural light, the building operated as a sort of sensory deprivation tank. Maybe the world outside had ended, and she was the last woman alive?

Would that be so bad? No people meant no racist, shit-for-brains cops. She could go wherever she wanted, and not get turned away or insulted because of the color of her skin. It sounded positively utopian. She could sleep in the best penthouses in Manhattan, a different one every night. She could go to the Natural History Museum and wander around the exhibits undisturbed, without security following her. And she could visit the nearest police station, squat in the doorway, and drop a—

Voices, far above her. Hart's deep baritone boomed ethereally from upstairs.

Okay, so maybe she wasn't the last person alive. But that was fine. She supposed she'd get bored with her own company after a while.

When she reached the third floor, she stopped. The light from her candle did little to lift the oppressive black cloak of the corridor, but it did reveal hitherto unknown details, such as the unsanded wooden floor and the exposed brick of the walls. An object glinted at the edge of the soft light thrown by the flickering candle, and she crouched to inspect it.

There, half-buried beneath layers of dust and rat turds, was a wrench. It must have been left by the builders when the project was unceremoniously abandoned. She picked the tool up and wondered what other weapons she might find, then decided against searching any further. She had a light, and a weapon, and that was enough.

Turning her back on the corridor, Foxy walked towards the stairs and began her ascent. She took the steps two at a time, slowing only when the flame of her candle wavered.

"Stay cool," she whispered, cupping her hand around the flame. "Almost there."

The men's muffled voices grew louder.

Not long now.

She took three more steps and arrived at the top of the stairs. So where *were* the men? Had they reached the roof? If so, there must be a trapdoor, or a hatch, or some way to—

Then she spotted it.

At the far end of the corridor, near the disused second staircase... a shaft of pale blue light flooding in from a trap-door-shaped gap in the ceiling. She had almost made it. Now all she needed to do was walk the length of the corridor to reach the entrance to the roof.

"Oh, gimme a fucking break," she sighed, less than thrilled at the prospect of traversing the dank hallway, passing door after door where some lurking terror could shamble out at her. But what choice did she have? The men had made it just fine, presumably. Okay, so there were five of them, along with Martha and Daniella, and possibly even *more* people if they picked anyone up on the way... but still, if they could do it, so could she. Plus, she was armed now, and the shaft of light offered a reassuring endpoint to aim for.

As she swallowed her fear, Foxy thought about Candy. Was her friend still alive? She hoped so. And as she started along the corridor, following the moonlight, the wrench clutched tightly in her hand, she realized that hope was all she had left.

**29**

---

Candy plunged further into the abyss.

She hurried down the stairs, the pain in her broken foot ebbing away to nothing as instinct took over, afraid that if she stopped, she would never reach the end.

If there even *was* an end.

She kept counting as she ran, eventually losing track somewhere around one hundred, when she heard the thing following her, its footsteps echoing malevolently and mirroring the frantic beating of her poor, overworked heart.

Sandra's voice no longer called to her, but that was okay, because Candy knew now that Sandra was long dead.

"Just kill me!" she screamed into the void. "Get it over with!"

Was she destined to descend these stairs forever, until her heart finally gave up and burst? She didn't deserve this. No one did. Sure, she had killed a priest on holy ground, but in self-defense. He was going to murder her. Worse, in fact. He had put a knife inside her. And all for his god, in whose name so much blood had already been spilled over the centuries.

Well, fuck his god. And fuck him, too. She would outrun them both. She would keep going, down and down, spiraling into insanity before allowing—

She tripped.

One of the steps — doubtlessly by design rather than accident — was lower than the others, and she fell forwards, bringing her arms up to her face to protect her head. Bracing herself for the impact of several sharp stairs against her body, she was surprised when she smacked onto flat ground. Her knees absorbed the worst of the fall, and she quickly scrambled backwards until her spine struck a moss-coated brick wall. Water dribbled between cracks in the masonry, staining the walls a dark, fecal brown.

"Oh my god," she gasped, as the room gradually swam into focus and she realized she could see again.

Ahead of her stood a wooden staircase, worn and splitting from decades of use. She counted the steps. Ten of them, leading to a metal door. A furnace rumbled ominously nearby, though somehow it radiated a frigid chill.

The basement.

She had made it. It was different than before, though. The stacked pews and bibles were absent, and the wooden crucifix was nowhere to be seen. She glanced up at the light bulb, which swayed gently from side to side.

With great care, Candy got to her feet. She looked down at her clothes. The dress she had borrowed from Sandra was stained a filthy black. She thought of the girl, who was almost certainly dead, and cried. What the fuck was going on?

Candy headed towards the stairs with mounting dread, laying her hand on the rail. It felt real. She was sure it wasn't a dream. Counting in her head as she did so, she climbed.

*One... two... three...*

The light remained on, casting her shadow against the steps.

*Four... five... six...*

Was it her imagination, or was the door ajar?

*Seven... eight... nine...*

She took the last step quickly and hesitated before the unlocked door. After one final glance into the basement, Candy placed her palm against the metal and pushed the door open, unprepared for the nightmare that awaited her.

**30**

———

Martha had only ever been on the roof once before.

On the day she had purchased the useless building, she had walked each floor with a clipboard and pencil, checking the rooms and making a note of the bare minimum she would need to purchase in order to turn the unfinished factory into a functioning brothel. Initially, she had grand plans of renovating the upper two floors, but so far, wary of attracting excessive police attention, levels three and four had remained untouched.

Now she wondered if she would ever get the chance. The lower levels were a slaughterhouse. Dead bodies strewn around like discarded playthings, the corridors awash with blood and entrails. Was there any coming back from this?

Possibly.

She doubted word of the evening's events would spread. Men were unlikely to disclose their nocturnal visits to friends and family, and everyone present seemed to want to forget the whole thing had ever happened. Certainly, no one desired police involvement. She would lose them all as customers, that was for sure... but if she closed for a week —

no, for four days — then a damn good scrub, a fresh coat of paint, and some clean linens would make everything nice and new. No one would ever have to know.

As for the bodies? Well, there was always the furnace.

Her biggest problem, as far as she could tell, was Candy. Could she buy the girl's silence? She thought so. The little bitch owed her, big time. Hell, she'd even give her back her job. And if she refused... *there was always that furnace.*

"No," she moaned softly. What was she thinking? That she could kill Candy and burn her body? Martha was a cold, hard woman — she'd had to be to survive — but she wasn't a murderer. She had to face facts.

It was all over.

She watched the men knot the bloodstained sheets into a makeshift rope. Behind them, the lights of the city sparkled in the night, black smoke rising from some unknown blaze in the distance. Hart paced back and forth, ordering people around, making sure no one was slacking. He was in charge now, not her. Her reign had come to an end. A boat on the river sounded its lonesome horn, and for the first time since she was a child, Martha felt like crying.

She stared out over the city; at the disused tire factory, and the abandoned warehouse, and the closed-down deli on the corner. Nothing lasted forever, she supposed. She should have burned this infernal place to the ground years ago and collected the insurance. Then she could have headed for pastures new, perhaps a small town in the south, and—

"Oh my god," said Daniella, snapping Martha from her thoughts. "Look at that."

Martha wearily rubbed at her eyes. "Look at what?"

"*That!*" shrieked the girl. "The building. It's—"

She didn't have to finish the sentence. The abandoned

warehouse opposite the brothel was shifting, as if it rested atop a choppy sea. What the hell was happening now? A quake?

The warehouse seemed to fold in on itself, beams splintering with ear-splitting cracks. The men stopped working.

"What's going on?" Hart called over.

*Quake,* Martha wanted to reply, but she couldn't get the words out, for as the warehouse crumbled to ruin, it revealed a trail of devastation that spread across the city as far as her eyes could see. Buildings had toppled in a straight line of carnage that appeared to be heading directly for—

"Oh shit," she managed to whisper.

That was no fault line. It was too perfect, too direct. She stared at the street, watching as it billowed, the concrete bulging.

"Hurry," she said to Hart. "Fucking *hurry!*"

"What is it?"

She glanced back down. "The whole building's gonna fall."

Hart stood, frozen, as the dust cloud rose from the warehouse. "Holy mother of god," he said, then turned to the men. "Alright, come on! It's long enough. Let's get out of here. Tie it to that," he said, pointing towards the sizeable air con unit that sat near the edge of the building.

"You think it'll hold?" asked the man in the tweed suit.

"It'll hold," said Hart, though he didn't sound convinced.

Martha only half paid attention. She was too busy studying the street, as the cracks in the road made their way, snake-like, towards the brothel. What was happening? There had to be something under the ground, digging it up. But what? What the hell could *do* that?

Hart checked the tautness of the rope, yanking on it. "Secure," he said. "I'll go—"

But one of the men was ahead of him. It was Foxy's client, a well-groomed man who was clearly dressed incognito, with sunglasses and a baseball cap. He elbowed past Hart and grabbed the rope, hurriedly lowering himself down.

"Motherfucker," snarled Hart, pulling Martha's small pistol from his waistband. He leaned over the edge and pointed the weapon. Martha and Daniella joined him, watching as the man descended.

Another of the clients, who went by the name of Mickey, and who Martha knew was a cheapskate who never left a tip, grabbed the hastily constructed cord, ready to follow.

"One at a time," barked Hart. "It won't hold two of us." He turned to Martha. "Keep an eye out for the cops."

"I think they'll be busy," she muttered, listening to the sirens and looking out over the ruined buildings. She went back to watching Foxy's client escape. He was halfway down the building now, using the knots in the sheets to rest his feet on.

Beneath him, the ground shuddered.

"It's happening," said Martha. Should she jump? Would that be better than the irony of being buried under the rubble of her own damn whorehouse?

The concrete bubbled, splitting open like a Venus fly trap. Martha squinted into the darkness. Her legs buckled, and she had to grip onto the edge to stop herself from falling.

Something was coming out of the ground. Two limbs, black and wizened by time, erupted from the widening crack.

"We're fucked," said Martha. Had the men noticed? Was anyone else seeing what she was fucking seeing? She looked at Hart. He took a step back, and caught her eye.

"What *is* that?" he said, as more splits appeared in the road, more arms digging and clawing at the ground. At first, Martha thought they were some sort of unknown alien creature. But as the desiccated figures shambled free of their concrete prison, she saw they were human.

Or had been, once.

Their ancient, tortured bodies bore the ravages of time, skeletal limbs with ragged cloth hanging over withered, fleshless frames. Some looked fresher than others, decaying flesh stretched taut over angular skulls like a funeral shroud made of the finest lace.

Foxy's client was unaware. He was almost at the end of the rope. He looked up at the onlookers, gave a quick thumbs up, and let go, falling the remaining five or six feet.

The corpses — for what else could they be? — were on him immediately.

Four of them crowded him, their limbs swinging wildly. He had enough time to scream, before they knocked him to the ground, each grabbing an arm or leg, pulling, the man's shrieks rising to a reedy wail. His left leg was the first to go. It tore from his body with a ghastly ripping sound, dark blood flooding from the wound and pooling in the gutter. The creature tossed the limb aside.

The brothel suddenly lurched, tilting at an angle. Mickey, who had been leaning furthest over the edge, lost his balance. He tumbled over the side, landing headfirst on the sidewalk. His head burst in a juicy explosion of crimson gore, his limbs dancing frenziedly for several seconds as the creatures from below slashed at the first man, tearing his clothes and ripping his skin to shreds.

Hart took a shot, the bullet thudding into one of the decrepit figures in a puff of smoke.

"They're dead," whispered Martha.

"What did you say?" roared Hart.

"You can't shoot them," she said, louder this time. "They're already dead."

"You're crazy, bitch," he said, and fired again.

More and more of the ghouls were appearing from the ground. Dozens of them. *Hundreds.* One rotting nightmare crawled out in a veil and wedding dress, several ribs bursting through the stained fabric.

But it was the children that haunted Martha the most. The children in their funeral suits, their hair lank and matted with dirt, small fingers bleeding and crooked and broken from digging.

Daniella was screaming, the men backing away, as the horrific gathering tilted their heads up, their blank, hollow eye sockets nothing more than black pools of malevolence.

Then, the first of them dug its nails into the wall and started to climb.

"It's impossible," said Hart, as the other creatures followed. "Fucking impossible."

The two remaining men looked to Hart for guidance, like children to an adult, unsure of what to do. Martha wanted to grab Daniella and slap her, shut her up for a second, and she, too, found herself waiting for Hart to make the next move. She didn't have to wait long. When the first rotten hand smacked dustily down on the roof, Hart turned and ran for the open hatch.

The old tenants of the Manhattan Riverfront Church had returned.

~

Foxy heard the gunshots.

She heard the screams.

She heard it all, and yet she kept walking down the corridor, for it was her only way out, and she reasoned that whatever was out there couldn't possibly be worse than what was inside. Unless the thing that stalked the halls had somehow reached the roof? Even so, she had to take the chance.

Forty feet from the hatch, she slowed as a shadow appeared, momentarily blocking the moonlight. A body leaped down into the darkness, thudded against the wall, and made for the nearest staircase. Foxy couldn't say definitively, but judging by the size of the figure, it was most likely Hart.

The idea scared her. Hart was the very last person she would expect to see fleeing the scene. He was a big man, an ex-con with a fearsome temper and a penchant for violence, who backed down from no one. Another body followed, scrambling through, their gown catching on something. Martha. The woman hung there until her gown tore, then landed badly on one leg. Foxy heard the woman's ankle break from the other end of the corridor.

Instinctively, she blew her candle out.

A third person tumbled through the gap. Foxy couldn't make out who it was. The figure landed next to Martha.

"Help me," Martha panted. "My ankle—"

"Fottiti la caviglia," said Daniella, and ran for the stairs, following Hart's lead.

"Wait!" screamed Martha. "I'll pay you! I have money! I have…"

Foxy took a step back. Something was very wrong. But there had to still be several men on the roof. Maybe they had wrestled the gun from Hart and tried to shoot him? Foxy's mind whirred with possibilities, until one of the men appeared at the hatch. He seemed to be fighting his way out, only his arms and head visible as he tried to go through headfirst. It was a sure way to break his neck, Foxy thought, as he stretched and reached for Martha.

"What are they?" he screamed. "What the fuck are—"

His words were cut short. His arms stiffened, fingers grasping at thin air before loosening, his head slumping as he slid forwards in silhouette and slammed to the floor. It took Foxy a second to understand what had happened.

His legs were gone.

Only his upper torso had made it through. Blood poured, splattering noisily onto the floor in a relentless torrent.

Foxy gripped the wrench in a trembling fist and started backing away. When more bodies — hideous, misshapen bodies — dropped through the gap, she turned and ran. She didn't know who they were. She didn't know *what* they were. But she understood one thing — they wanted to kill her.

Martha shielded herself from the blood. It poured in frothing waves, drenching her. She tried to stand, but in the dim moonlight she saw a bone jutting out of her ankle at a gruesome angle, the skin around it frayed.

A face leered at her through the hatch.

The creature tumbled through, landing on its back. The impact would have broken a normal person's spine... but not a dead man's. Dry bones snapped into place with audible clicks and pops as the twisted body simply unfolded itself.

"Fuck you," said Martha. "You rotten, dead *fuck.*"

Then it was on her, biting and tearing, its hands clawing at her flesh. Ragged nails raked down her cheeks, gashing them open. She screamed as a rancid hand groped inside her mouth, the gnarled fingers clamping round her tongue. They closed tight, squeezing the organ, even as she bit down on the wrist. It tasted of the grave, her teeth meeting bony resistance, as the creature tightened its grip, squashing her tongue until flattened muscle slid between its vile fingers, blood filling her mouth and spilling out. It wrenched the pink organ free with brute strength and hurled it against the wall with a loud splat, and as Martha died, more and more of the cemetery denizens filed in, crawling over each other in their desperate bid to reclaim what was once theirs and would be again.

**31**

―――――

CANDY STEPPED THROUGH THE DOOR INTO THE CORRIDOR. Except it wasn't the corridor she was expecting. It was different. Grander, more elegant, with wooden flooring, and arched doorways with intricate carvings on the panels. Though the lights were dim, she noticed the walls were painted a pale green, with paintings depicting religious iconography hanging between the doors. She took a closer look at one.

In the painting, a withered Jesus drooped from the cross, splashes of blood running down his legs while onlookers booed and jeered him. With typical inaccuracy, he was a white man, and wearing nothing but absurdly anachronistic bikini briefs. He was cleanly shaven, with feminine features that—

Candy rubbed at her eyes.

She was seeing things. It couldn't be.

The Christ figure in the picture wasn't Jesus. It was *her*. She hung there, half-naked, her face — a chilling likeness, she had to concede — screaming in tortured agony.

"Fuck that," she whispered, then turned away and stumbled down the corridor, groaning each time she put her weight on her foot. Where was she going? Hell, where *was* she? She didn't know. But there had to be a way out somewhere.

There simply *had* to be.

Daniella hurtled down the stairs, screaming all the way. The lights were off, but she could hear — god, she could still *hear* — Martha's tortured wails, and the rending of flesh, the snapping of bone.

What the fuck *were* those things?

"Wait!" she called to Hart, barely recognizing the panicky voice as her own. He had the gun, dammit! He had the gun, and yet he was the first to hightail it off the roof. *"Fottuto codardo!"* She was short of breath, and stopped screaming, using her lungs for their intended purpose.

Footsteps clattered above her. They were too fast. The noise was deafening, hundreds of feet and hands smacking off the steps. She imagined them crawling over each other like maggots, wriggling and tumbling in pursuit.

She peered over the balcony and saw Hart below her, puffing his way down. If she hurried, she would catch him. She increased her pace, jumping the last three steps, holding onto the rail to stay upright as she took the corner sharply.

They had been so close to escaping. A couple of minutes earlier, and they might have made it down before those... *things* arrived. But they had spent too long arguing, too long fighting amongst themselves. And now they were all going to die.

Ahead of her, Hart had stopped to cough. The big man

was out of breath, and almost within touching distance. Daniella barreled after him. She drew level and stepped around him with nimble feet. Ballerina's feet, her mother had always called them.

"Shoot them!" she shouted as she reached the final flight of stairs. "Shoot them all!"

Hart glanced up at her, nodded, and pulled the trigger.

A sharp report echoed throughout the staircase. Daniella kept running. She couldn't slow down, not if—

She slumped against the wall, smacking her head off the plaster. What had happened? She tried to stand, but an agonizing pain sliced through her. Blood. There was blood on her stomach. She could see it pumping out of the wound, the *bullet* wound, a scarlet rainbow spraying across the stairs with each beat of her heart. As Hart passed her, she looked up at him with tears in her eyes.

"You shot me," she whimpered.

"Nothing personal, baby," he said, and carried on without her, muttering, "But they ain't gonna get *me*."

She watched him go. Above her, the creatures continued their descent. Daniella hooked her fingers over the nearest step, dragging herself forwards. She rolled down, thudding painfully down the staircase, trying to curl herself into a ball. She landed at the bottom, sprawled out, blood gushing from her torso. Hart was gone, and she was all alone.

Well... not quite *alone*.

The dead people never paused, an avalanche of corpses thrashing down the steps towards her. The smell hit her first, the stench of ancient tombs, of interred bodies, of rotted limbs and worm-riddled skulls. Vomit rose in her throat, but before she could eject it, they were on her. They scratched and bit, her tanned flesh offering no resistance to the freewheeling chaos of bodies. Her clothes were first to go, shredded by multiple hands, and with that barrier gone, her skin was next. They burrowed into her belly, tearing through the flesh, hands churning her guts, the creatures not stopping, treading all over her, each taking their turn to mutilate her. A thumb pressed into her eyeball, the orb erupting in thick goo as two bony fingers caught in her nostrils, breaking her nose, tearing it from her face. She tried to fight, but her limbs were pinned under the weight of so many corpses. Soon, her ribcage gave way, the creatures continuing on their dreadful journey, treating her as merely an obstacle to be quickly overcome, and by the time they had passed Daniella, there was nothing left of her but a flattened, sticky paste at the bottom of the stairs.

Something was following Foxy.

Thin, bony feet cracked drily off the floor like firecrackers. She turned her head, glancing at the shambling ghoul advancing towards her, eerily backlit by the shaft of moonlight through the open hatch.

It was gaining on her.

How close to the staircase was she? She looked ahead. It was an *eternity* away. Sharp fingers clawed at her shoulder, and she ducked through the nearest doorway. The thing chasing her skidded, overshooting the mark, and Foxy had just enough time to ready the wrench in her hand for when it emerged around the—

No, not enough time. The creature lunged. Foxy swung, but already it was atop her, the wrench slipping from her grasp and whistling through the air. A foul odor assailed her nostrils as frantic hands scratched at her face. She wrapped her own fingers around the creature's neck, horrified to discover it *had* no neck, just a dusty spinal column.

*What are you,* she wanted to scream, but Foxy's finely honed survival instinct told her not to. The rest of the strange brood had followed Hart and Daniella down the far staircase, and to scream would be to potentially alert them. And so she kept quiet, sliding her hands up the barren backbone towards the head, or what remained of it. Never before had Foxy been so thankful for the deceptive power of the darkness, for to see the face of her attacker would surely drive her to the brink of insanity. Her thumb pressed against the jaw, loose, flaking skin sagging over her hand, and she stabbed through the gossamer-fine flesh, her fist disappearing through the jaw, nails scraping against the palate. Then, with a strength borne of oncoming madness, she snapped the head backwards, the spine crumbling to dust and raining tiny shards over her.

The dead person's skull hit the floor, disintegrating on contact, before the limp body collapsed on top of her, its cracked ribs jabbing into Foxy's stomach. She shoved the corpse aside and brushed her hands against her skirt to remove the residue of death.

Were there more of them? Had they heard the struggle? She crawled through the room, sweeping her hand in front of her until she found the wrench, snatching it up and clutching it to her chest as she listened, her heart pounding through her waistcoat, hard enough to make her arms vibrate.

Raising the wrench like a baseball bat, she peeked around the door frame and scanned the hallway.

Nothing there, save what appeared to be Martha's shredded remains.

This was it. Her chance to escape. With those... *things*

following Hart downstairs, she could reach the roof and climb down... or at least signal for help. She took a bold step forwards, leaving the dead creature in the room. There was no time to—

At the far end of the corridor, a misshapen, darkened head snapped up from where it had been feasting on Martha's innards. It rose, ill-fitting clothes draped shapelessly over a horrifying, impossibly scrawny frame. Blood dripped from its fingertips into an ever-widening pool of viscera.

That was okay. She had killed one of them already. As long as it was a one-on-one encounter, she figured she could handle it.

The creature stumbled forwards and let its jaw drop, emitting a blood-curdling shriek so loud that Foxy felt it rumble in her stomach.

"Oh fuck," she whispered, as the high-pitched wail continued unabated.

The creature quietened. Then, seconds later, its call was met by dozens of nightmarish responses.

Foxy stepped backwards, gripping her weapon.

"Oh, fuck, fuck, *fuck*," she said.

This was it.

They were coming.

**32**

─────────

Candy averted her eyes from the paintings as she passed them, keeping her gaze set dead center. The image of her own face, of her own crucified body, haunted her. What did it mean?

Part of her knew she wasn't getting out of this alive, and that every step she took only delayed the inevitable. Should she just sit down and close her eyes and let death overcome her?

*Everyone dies,* she reasoned. *So why not get it over with?*

But something deep inside kept her going. The survival instinct of the human spirit could be crushed, seemingly beyond repair... but never fully destroyed. It was always there, offering hope, or desperation, or a queasy mixture of the two.

Sweat dripped down her brow, and she wiped it away. It was uncomfortably hot in here, and getting warmer with each step.

*You're in hell.*

No. She didn't believe in heaven, so she sure as shit didn't believe in hell. At least, not in the biblical sense. Hell was having to choose between paying rent or eating. Hell was being assaulted by a crazed priest. Hell was being trapped in a brothel by religious wackos with murder on their minds.

Hell was New York City, with its muggers and crackheads and rapists and killers. She dealt with that every day, and she could deal with this... whatever *this* was. She turned back to see how far she had come, but there was nothing there, not anymore. Just a hopeless, empty void.

The end of all things.

She resumed walking, expecting each doorway she passed to burst open and reveal some new hidden atrocity. They never did. She was being deliberately led somewhere, but by whom, and for what ghoulish purpose, she did not know.

At the end of the corridor stood an enormous wooden door, thick black smoke billowing from under it. This was it. The epicenter, a place of twisted, spiraling evil. A light wind caressed her, urging her onwards. It was unnecessary. She understood beyond all doubt that there was no going back now.

Gingerly placing her hand on the ornate brass handle, she felt heat radiating through the door, and suddenly she knew exactly what she would find on the other side. She knew, because she had seen it before.

In the basement.

"Now or never," she whispered, and pushed the portal — for it was more than a door, she realized — open. It groaned on tired hinges, gasping lethargically and revealing the interior of the Manhattan Riverfront Church. It was as Candy remembered it from her ghastly vision.

Flames licked the walls, incinerating curtains with holy symbols stitched on them, while broken shards from the stained glass window sparkled in the flickering light of the fire. Candy walked inside, stumbling over the corpse of a nude woman whose crushed head resembled the remains of a popped party balloon.

She stepped over the body and gazed at the conflagration engulfing the church. A man sat in one of the pews, seemingly untouched by the blaze. He stared ahead at a featureless wooden cross that balanced before the pulpit. The fire danced around it, impotently threatening the flammable object.

It was all as she remembered it. The heat, the confusion, the terror.

She looked to the man, and he was standing now, turning to face her, a bible clutched feverishly in his hands.

The priest acknowledged her with a nod.

"Welcome, sinner," he said, and smiled. "Welcome to *hell.*"

**33**

———

Colt navigated the Mustang through the darkened streets. It was pouring rain, and he jammed the wipers on. It did no good, however, for this was not a normal downpour.

Tonight, in Manhattan, it was raining blood.

Huge droplets pounded the windshield, the wipers smearing it across the glass like a macabre rainbow.

Maroney sat silently in the passenger seat. The carnage outside was absolute, entire blocks lying in ruin, their fires lighting up the night sky. From all around came hopeless, despairing screams.

"Break the windshield," said Colt. Maroney only looked at him. "*Do it.* I can't see a damned thing."

Maroney unclipped his service revolver and smacked it hard against the window. It took three blows before it cracked. Then the younger man leaned back in his seat, aimed the soles of his boots, and kicked the glass out. Shards dropped into the vehicle, blood from the skies splashing across the dashboard and steering wheel.

"This can't be happening, man," mumbled Maroney. "This isn't real."

Colt shrugged and kept his eyes on the road. They didn't have far to go.

The old site of the Manhattan Riverfront Church was only a couple of blocks away.

~

Foxy hit the stairs running.

They were behind her, following, and a goddam wrench wasn't gonna stop them. The corpses were fast, but so was she, and, having spent the last few years having sex multiple times per night, her cardio was not an issue.

As she arrived at the third level, she wondered what she would do when she reached the bottom. The doors were chained, there were no windows, and she smelled smoke. Thick, belching smoke, like the building was on fire. She was so utterly fucked that she felt like laughing.

*Out of the frying pan, and into the literal fire.*

The lights on level two were still on, casting a welcome glow over the stairs. Somehow, she found the strength to speed up. She tried to think of a place to hide. What about the cubicles in the locker room? No, that wouldn't do. It was possible to climb over the doors. Foxy knew this all too well, remembering the time she had gotten stuck in one of them and had to stand on the toilet and scramble over the top.

The air rippled behind her as something swiped at her hair. She spun, swinging the wrench at her attacker and aiming too high, the weapon going clean over the creature's head.

As Foxy overbalanced, she realized why she had missed.

The creature was only a child.

She fell backwards, jolting her spine on the stairs, and the little dead boy leaped upon her. He could be no older than ten, his barren face pockmarked with holes from which fat, pale worms dangled. He clawed at her, his face inches away, and widened his jaw to take a bite out of her nose. A mouthful of maggots spilled from between his lips, and Foxy gagged as the wriggling beasts entered her own mouth.

The child's small fingers scratched at her, his rotten nails failing to break the skin. Foxy raised the wrench and brought it screaming down on his head. It burst through the cranium at an angle, smashing into the soft skull and erupting from the other side in a cloud of ethereal dust. The boy went stiff... and then fell, the wrench clanging off the stairs. Foxy slipped out from under him, rolled onto her hands and knees, and threw up. The maggots writhed in her vomit, as above her, dozens of feet pounded the stairs.

More of them. Too many.

Foxy — who was not given to tears — wept as she stood.

"I'll kill you all if I have to, motherfuckers," she half-sobbed, half-screamed. Then she reached down, plucked the wrench from the back of the little boy's head, and carried on down the stairs with the taste of death lingering in her throat.

"Slow down, you're gonna get us killed!" yelled Maroney.

Colt ignored him. This was a race against time. The blood kept raining down, turning the hood of the car a bright red. The wheels skidded on the slick road, and he sideswiped a parked vehicle before regaining control.

Colt knew the brothel well. He had tried to bust it when they first opened many years ago, until Martha had offered him his pick of the girls two nights per week. It was one of the perks of the job, though since he had thrown his back out a couple of years earlier, he hadn't visited as often. And even when he had, the place always had a weird atmosphere. At first he thought it was the lack of windows, or the constant hum of the air con. But it was more than that. The building gave off... bad vibrations. He didn't know how else to put it.

He wondered if the tunnelers had arrived at their destination yet. What would happen once they did? Colt doubted it would be anything good. And anyway, he would soon find out.

The brothel was less than a minute away.

**34**

———

The fucking priest.

Candy knew it would be, despite the impossible knowledge that she had killed him and stuffed his body into an incinerator earlier that evening. He looked different now, standing before her, his skin unmarred by the burns that had covered him previously.

"I've been waiting for you," he said. "Waiting an eternity, forced to stand helplessly by and watch my church, my *sanctuary,* burn to the ground. Until tonight. Until you came."

"You're dead," said Candy, surprised she could even force the words out. "I killed you."

"A necessary sacrifice, whore. Our Lord in Heaven blessed mankind with his resurrection a long time ago. He did it to save our souls, and now I, in turn, make my own feeble gesture in tribute."

A tremor from behind him. The old wooden cross... it was *moving*. It seemed to float through the raging flames, gliding towards the priest. He stepped aside reverentially, allowing it passage.

"I'll kill you again," said Candy. "I swear it."

The priest wore a satisfied smirk and began leafing through the pages of his bible.

The old cross continued on with dreadful inevitability. Candy took several steps back, the fire forming an impenetrable wall on both sides.

The cross was coming for her.

She thought of the painting in the hallway, so lifelike, so awful, and felt her sanity drain away. She was surprised it had lasted this long. But then, she hadn't had *time* to stop and ponder the abominable goings on.

She backed up further, tears in her wretched eyes, and then two firm hands grasped her shoulders. She shook free and spun to face her assailant. The dead woman from the doorway stood there, her broken skull rattling around in the soft sack of flesh that drooped from her neck down over her chest.

Candy screamed.

That was it. The final straw. It was too much, too much, too much. The terror and the insanity of it all. She screamed, and she screamed, and as the dead woman advanced, her smashed head swaying back and forth across her breasts, blood leaking down her nude body, Candy could do nothing but walk backwards in abject horror.

"Pray!" shouted the priest. "Pray for your sins! Get down on your knees and beg for salvation before it's too late!"

The dead woman's arms stretched out blindly towards her.

"Why?" screamed Candy. "Why are you doing this?"

"The dawn of a new age is upon us," said the priest. "The end of sin, when the wicked shall be washed away in a river of blood!"

With nowhere left to run, Candy thudded into the cross, the fire raging all around her.

"The Savior has been reborn," ranted the priest.

Pressed up against the cross, Candy looked beyond the slaughtered woman at the doorway. Celestial white light flooded in, and in its mighty beam stood an appalling silhouette.

The priest raised his bible to the sky.

*"Once more,"* he cried, *"Jesus Christ walks the Earth!"*

"No, no, no," sobbed Candy, as the carved Jesus, dark and misshapen, staggered out of the light and down the aisle.

The last time she had seen the wooden monstrosity, it had been attached to the very cross that currently pressed up against her. Now it was free, free to roam, to hunt, to *kill*. The gnarled body creaked with each step, the long spikes that had held it in place jutting obscenely through its palms, human skin draped over its face and shoulders.

Sandra's skin.

"No!" screamed Candy. *"No!"*

"He walks! He lives! Worship at his feet!"

The holy idol approached, Sandra's death mask slipping to the side, revealing the weathered, distorted countenance of the carved Christ, its mouth locked in an eternal grimace. It shoved the dead woman aside, casting her into the flames, and came for Candy. She raised her arms in defense, and the wooden Jesus plunged its nails into her wrists. Hot blood fountained from the wounds as the Christ-figure spread her arms apart and rammed the nails into the cross.

Candy looked into its eyes. They were bottomless pits of despair. She tried to wish away the small part of her that still desperately clung to her useless, unwanted sanity.

"It is time!" cried the priest. "Complete the blood sacrifice!"

The carved Jesus wrenched its hands away, leaving the

nails in Candy's wrists, pinning her to the cross. Sandra's loose skin slipped fully from the face, splatting wetly to the carpeted floor.

Candy shook her head uncontrollably as her lifeblood spurted from her wounds. The image of the painting flashed once more into her mind, and she closed her eyes, welcoming madness, begging for it.

"*I am against you,*" said the priest as he read from his bible. "*I will pull up your dress over your face! I will show your nakedness to the nations, and your disgrace to the kingdoms!*"

He tore the blood-soaked summer dress from her body.

"*I will hurl abominable filth upon you, making you look foolish!*"

Her panties were next, savagely ripped away, leaving her naked.

"*I will make an example of you!*"

She hung there, crucified and screaming, as the priest's bible burst into black flame.

"Nahun, 3:6," he said, then turned to the wooden Jesus. "*Innumerable are the harlotries of this well-favored whore, this mistress of witchcraft who enslaves nations through her fornication!*"

"Get it over with!" Candy screamed in response. "Just fucking kill me!"

"That's right!" said the priest. "Tremble before God's holy vessel! He will be reborn through you!"

She tried to think of something, anything, to transport her from the miserable unreality of the church. How much longer could this diabolical charade go on for?

The Christ came for her, wrapping its grotesque fingers around her throat, red lights twinkling evilly in the black craters of its eyes. Candy knew that look. She had seen it before, hundreds of times, in the eyes of her clients as they licked their lips and glared lasciviously at her... and suddenly she was afraid that death was not the worst thing that was going to happen to her.

The carved Christ moved closer. Rigid hands roughly caressed her face, the thumb scratching at her lips.

"What are you doing?" asked Candy, as she hung from the cross, distressingly aware of her nakedness. She looked to the priest. *"What's it doing?"*

The priest's pompous expression faltered. "Yes, My Lord," he said. "Witness the vulgar pleasures of the flesh. This corruption is what we must battle! The very fate of mankind is at stake. Strike her down and bring about the new age of Christ!"

The wooden Jesus placed one hand on her breast and squeezed it tightly. Candy cried out in pain as it massaged the handful with coarse digits.

"Stop," wept Candy. "God, stop!"

It stared at her, the crimson orbs in its eye sockets growing larger, more intense, and put its face to her neck, rubbing the craggy hardness of the mouth against her. The wood snagged on her skin, cutting her.

"Okay, My Lord," said the priest. "That will be all. We have a righteous mission to attend to."

But the holy idol wasn't listening. Its eyes blazed with infernal lust for Candy's unclad body as it ran uneven hands over her flesh.

"Please, we have work to do," the priest uttered, though his confidence appeared to have deserted him. The wooden Jesus turned away from Candy, staring at the holy man, its eyes burning so brightly that they dimmed the raging inferno that surrounded them. The priest placed a delicate hand on the carving's shoulder. "Come. Soon, the fire will consume this holy sanctuary. We must be gone before it consumes us, too."

The wooden Jesus seemed to be thinking, the hands remaining firm on Candy's breasts. The fire burned all around the trio, close enough to singe the hairs on her arms.

"It's dangerous for you here!" roared the priest. "We must leave."

*Dangerous,* thought Candy. *It's dangerous for you here.*

The pressure on her breasts eased as the Jesus stepped backwards. The priest wiped sweat from his brow, a relieved expression settling over his features.

"Kill the whore," he whispered. *"Kill it."*

*We must be gone before it consumes us, too.*

The words played over in Candy's mind until at last she understood.

For the final time, the holy effigy placed its hands around her throat.

"Wait," spluttered Candy. "Wait!"

The carved Christ stared at her. Through her half-lidded eyes, the statue was nothing but a blur. Blood gushed from her wrists. She took as deep a breath as her constricted larynx would allow, and forced a crooked smile.

"Be gentle, lover," she said. "Your touch..." She coughed up a mouthful of blood, then licked it from her lips. "... It feels so *good.*"

She knew she was dying. She didn't have long left.

The Jesus moved closer, its hard body touching hers.

"That's it, baby," she cooed. "That's it. Come to Candy. I'll make it all better."

The priest stormed towards them, beads of perspiration trickling down his forehead. "What are you doing? *Kill the whore!*"

"Don't listen to him, baby. I want you. You want me too,

don't you?" Her eyelids sagged, and she snapped her head up, fighting against her body's urge to give up.

"We're running out of time!" The priest grabbed the Jesus, spinning him around until they faced each other. "You have to—"

Wooden hands pressed onto the priest's temples, silencing him. With inhuman strength, they clamped shut, the holy man's jaw dropping open in a silent scream. Over the oppressive roar of the flames, Candy heard the man's skull cracking. Bloodshot eyeballs bulged from their sockets, white fluid and dark, dark blood weeping down his cheeks.

"It... was all... for you..." cried the priest, as more blood, flecked with tiny shards of splintered bone, gushed from his nostrils. One eye popped free from the socket, dangling by the optic nerve across his wet cheek. *"I... I love you!"*

They were his last words. The next second, his skull gave way, splitting apart under the immense power of the wooden Jesus. The carved hands clapped together, the priests's head bursting in an explosion of sloppy gore and brain matter, and then the priest spoke no more. His body toppled backwards into the fire, the flames greedily consuming him as the idol turned its attention back to Candy.

Her head had flopped down as an all-enveloping tiredness overcame her, and it took all her force of will to raise it and look at him. The mighty church door was still visible, though the flames were closing in, *gigantic* flames that towered over all in the hellish chapel.

The Christ looked over its shoulder at the exit, seeming to debate its next move. When it turned back to Candy, its engorged wooden penis swept through the blaze, catching fire. The tip burned white, then sparked into flames.

Candy knew what she had to do. She had to stop it leaving. She had to stop it from killing her and exiting the chapel. Nothing else mattered. Not her own pain and suffering. Not even her own life.

The Jesus approached, its phallus blazing mightily as the flames crept ever closer. The cross, too, was burning. It lapped at Candy's legs and back, and when the smell of sizzling hair follicles filled her nostrils, she realized her head was on fire.

"Come on, motherfucker," she roared. "Let's fucking do this!" She screwed her eyes shut, choking on black smoke and fumes, and when she opened them again and gazed directly into the red, maddening eyes of the Jesus, everything was okay, because she had completely lost her mind.

Her body went numb as she tore her arms free from the cross, leaving the thick, rusted nails embedded in the wood, and wrapped her bleeding limbs around the carved Christ's blazing torso.

And when the engorged, flaming phallus entered her, she felt no pain.

For Mary 'Candy' Holmes was no more.

She had simply ceased to exist.

**35**

———

The brothel was on fire.

Foxy took the last three steps with a jump and entered the reception area. Keeping below the toxic fumes, she dropped and crawled for the door. Maybe the protestors had unchained it?

*Why would they do that?*

She didn't know. Maybe they *just had*.

Smoke invaded her lungs and stung her eyes as the creatures pounded down the stairs. Holding her breath, she shuffled onwards, the door almost within reach. Her fingers grazed the metal, brushed its hard coolness... then something was pulling on her leg, dragging her away. She turned onto her back and swung the wrench blindly. There was a loud snap as the tool connected with bone, followed by the thud of a body hitting the floor.

More hands groped for her, withered fingers wrapping around her ankles, yanking her across the floor. Those bastards... they couldn't stop her now. Not when she was so close.

Foxy kicked free, thrashing her legs, and scrambled to

her feet. The smoke made visibility difficult, but that didn't matter. She knew where they were.

They were *everywhere*.

Shrieking like a banshee, Foxy readied the wrench, adjusted her stance, and went to work.

She brought the mighty weapon down on a lumbering silhouette, *hard,* cracking a skull. She swung again, breaking a creature's bone. Something slashed at her arm, gashing it open, and she threw a wild elbow, striking her assailant. They swarmed her like an undead plague, but Foxy was a woman possessed. The cocaine she had snorted flowed through her like God's holy light, her limbs buzzing with righteous fury.

Several came for her at once, overpowering her, forcing her onto the ground. With her free hand, she reached up to shove them away, and ancient teeth clamped down on her fingers, gnawing them to the bone. Foxy clenched her fist around the foul jaw and snapped it loose. Another of the ghouls bit at her thigh. She kicked it away, scrambling onto her knees and bringing the wrench crashing down on top of the creature's head.

"Fuck you!" she screamed, as she crushed another skull, listening to the satisfying reverberation of the metal wrench smashing off the floor. "Fuck you!"

Through the smoke, she saw a flickering light.

Fire.

It was coming from the basement, working its way up the wooden stairs. The advancing heat prickled her skin, and she knew she had to get out. Somehow, she *had* to get out. Ducking low again, she scurried towards the door, coughing on the fumes. It was hard to see in the darkness, the black smoke obscuring the dim hallway lights. She bumped into the metal door, shoved it, opened it... and it caught on the chain.

"No," she moaned quietly, shaking her head. The escape fantasy was over. She reached her arm through the gap, relishing the sensation of cool rain on her skin. Could she get her body through? Was it possible?

She pressed her head to the narrow opening, feeling the pressure on her temples, then closed her eyes and pushed. The rough edges of the doors cut into her skin, blood trickling down her face... but she was making progress. When she reached her ears, she screamed as the soft organs bent backwards, folding, the skin tearing.

Fuck it.

She abandoned the wrench, placed both hands on the doors, and yanked her head through. The pain was immense, but short-lived, for when Foxy opened her eyes and saw the street, and gasped in huge lungfuls of air, the joy of being almost free from the horrors inside overrode any physical trauma... at least until she saw what was happening.

The road was pockmarked with holes; large, human-sized tunnels that erupted from the asphalt. From somewhere nearby, a woman screamed. The scream competed with several police sirens and alarm systems. Streetlamps reflected off deep puddles, puddles that looked like...

Blood. It was *all* blood. It rained from the sky, it flooded the streets, it drummed against her face.

A car screeched round the corner at high speed, heading towards the building.

"Help!" yelled Foxy, though they were too far away to hear her. She waved her arm. *"Help me!"*

She felt faint. Only the cocaine was keeping her awake now.

*"Help me!"*

The car approached. It was red. All the cars were. And the buildings, and the streets...

"Help me, *please!*"

The temperature was unbearable, the fire raging out of control.

With all her might, Foxy tried to squeeze her body through the gap, but the space wasn't wide enough. She would have to cut off her own breasts to fit through.

The car was getting closer. Soon, it would pass her, and her only hope would be gone.

"Help me!" she screamed.

They had to see her.

Her life depended on it.

~

"There it is," said Colt, his jaw set.

The brothel loomed before them, a four-floor monument to the hubris of the man who had built it. A crooked streetlamp leaned against the side of the building, illuminating what appeared to be several terribly thin men clambering down the wall.

"Wait a fucking minute," said Colt, squinting through the shattered windshield. The men weren't *escaping* from the building. They were scaling the wall. They were climbing *in*.

Maroney had also spotted them. "I don't like this," said the younger man, his voice cracking. "I don't fucking *like this.*"

"Don't care," replied Colt. He narrowed his eyes, focusing on the brothel. The doors were partially ajar, and though black smoke belched through them in pulsing, billowing waves — just like on that terrible night, all those years ago — he saw something.

An arm, waving frantically, signaling to him.

A survivor.

He slammed his foot on the accelerator, heading straight for the doors, not noticing the holes in the road until Maroney yelled, "Look out!"

Colt spun the wheel to avoid the first of them. As he passed, he glanced down in disbelieving horror at the hands gripping the sides of the tunnel. Something was climbing out.

Despite his thirty years on the force, Colt's heart damn-near stopped. He thought he knew what to expect. He thought he was ready, that he was prepared. From a safe distance, he had witnessed the dead people in the tunnels, crawling, digging their way home... but to actually *see* a living corpse emerging from the ground, right before his wide, horrified eyes, shattered not only his entire belief system... but his sanity too.

Pain stabbed at his heart. He struggled to breathe, releasing the wheel and clutching at his chest, which felt obscenely full, like his heart was doubling in size with every labored gasp.

"Colt, watch out!" shouted Maroney. The younger officer lurched forwards to grab the wheel, the inertia on his seat-belt kicking in and preventing him from moving. And when one of the tunnelers emerged from the ground and hurled itself onto the hood of the car, Officer Maroney had one decision to make.

Go for the wheel... or go for his gun.

The car turned, heading towards the brothel.

Foxy kept waving, kept screaming for aid. They *had* to have seen her. Maybe they'd have something in the trunk to break the chains? A tire iron, or a shotgun... *anything.*

"Over here," she called out. "I'm stuck!" Thank god they had been passing. For once, her luck was in. She was...

Her hand dropped to her side when she realized what was happening.

"No... no..." she said.

The car was coming towards her, alright.

It was coming fast.

*Way* too fast.

"Oh shit," she said, her eyes widening as she saw the gaunt figure scrambling over the hood and through the broken windshield of the vehicle.

Panic hit her, and she tried to duck back through the gap. She pulled sharply, her ears catching on the doors, impeding her progress as she wriggled her head to free herself.

But it was no use.

She was stuck.

Maroney clutched his service revolver in his clammy hand, his body shaking with fear as he took the shot. The bullet tore through the thin man's shoulder as the vehicle juddered over the uneven surface.

It wasn't enough. The man — god, was it really a man? — scrambled further into the car, and Maroney watched helplessly as it sank its teeth into his partner's neck, tearing free a thick chunk of bloody flesh.

Colt slumped in his seat, his head lolling back, blood

spurting from torn arteries. His lifeless foot pressed hard on the pedal, the speedometer nudging sixty.

Maroney lined up a shot, aware he only had time for one more. The man turned to him, his face a mud-caked, grinning skull, and Maroney pulled the trigger.

This time his aim was true, and the bullet caught the dead man on the bridge of his nose. He tumbled to the side, rolling from the hood and hitting the tarmac in a crumpled heap of broken bones.

Maroney smiled a twisted, unhinged smile.

"Right between the eyes," he said, as a tear fell from his own.

He looked straight ahead at the terrified face of the girl stuck between the doors, raised his arms, and braced himself for impact.

Foxy was frozen. It was a sensation unlike any she had ever experienced. Time stopped, the out-of-control vehicle hurtling towards her in slow motion. She couldn't believe she was going to die here, trapped between the doors in Martha's fucking whorehouse.

All she could think about was how she hadn't spoken to her family in so long. So very fucking long. She would give anything to make one last call, to see them one last time, to hold her mom, to kiss her, to cry on her shoulder and be held, understood, and loved.

She stared into the bright, white lights of the headlamps, closed her eyes, and—

A hand on her ankle, gripping her tightly. No, *two* hands, violently tugging her through the doors. Her ears seemed to split, the lobes wrenched backwards as her mystery rescuer hauled her free, away from the door, depositing her back into the smoky reception area. The flames had reached the stairs, and now the entire lower corridor was ablaze. Foxy gazed up into the face of her rescuer.

"Get the fuck away from that door, cunt," snarled Hart. "Ain't no one getting out of here but me. I'm the one who—"

The doors exploded open.

A Mustang — once white, now drenched in blood — rocketed into the reception at sixty miles per hour, annihilating Hart where he stood. The vehicle cut him in two, his intestines splashing noisily across the hood as the Mustang roared past and slammed into the wall near the waiting area. Hart's upper torso whirled through the air before thumping to the floor in front of Foxy, as enormous cracks spread across the wall and ceiling, plaster crumbling overhead. The building rocked, huge chunks of masonry crashing down.

Foxy crawled as fast as she could towards the doors, Hart's lifeless eyes watching her all the way. Above her, support beams groaned.

She made it outside in time to turn back and watch the ceiling burst, stone and concrete giving way, the walls folding in on themselves as the flames rose higher and higher, seeming to scrape the moon. She crossed to the other side of the street in a daze, avoiding the holes that dotted the road, and collapsed against a parked car, watching as her place of work shuddered apocalyptically to the ground.

The rain had stopped, the rivers of blood slowly vanishing down the drains, as if they had never been there at all.

As if the whole thing had been a dream.

~

The ruins of Martha's brothel burned for seven days and nights. No matter how much water the firefighters doused it with, they could not control the blaze. Every time it appeared the battle was over, another flame would erupt from out of nowhere like weeds in a garden.

Then, at midnight on the seventh day, the fire abruptly ceased. The firefighters looked at each other in confusion, unsure of what they had done. It was as if someone had simply turned the gas off. They searched the rubble, more out of duty than belief. No one could have survived an inferno like that, they all agreed.

And it appeared that this time, they were correct.

**36**

---

It was past nine, and the streets were dark.

Foxy lingered in the shadows, a phantom with a cigarette burning between her fingers. Knowing that if she didn't go now, she *never* would, she started walking, leaving indistinct footprints in the light dusting of snow. Winter had arrived in the three weeks since the incident, and she hugged her leopard print coat tightly to her body, her breath steaming in front of her.

An earthquake.

That was how they had described it on the news; an earthquake that had traveled three miles in a straight line from Morningdale Cemetery to the riverfront, demolishing several city blocks on the way, and taking countless lives. Even now, authorities could only guess at the final death toll, and absolutely no one could account for the strange tunnels that had appeared around Martha's brothel that night.

Foxy could, of course, but she kept quiet about it. Who the hell would believe her? She stepped carefully around one of the holes, not daring to look inside, and reached a tall metal fence that circled the perimeter. It was covered with police tape and dire warnings of injury and death to trespassers. The snow was falling, and Foxy shivered as the microscopic flakes settled on her skin. She placed her hands on the barrier and peered at the remains, hoping that after tonight, the dreams would stop one and for all.

Every night since the fire, the nightmares had tormented her. Visions of Candy nailed to a cross, begging for help as the room slowly filled with blood. Was it guilt at not being able to save her friend? Foxy didn't know, and she never would — not unless she visited Candy's resting place and asked for forgiveness.

She scanned the ruins. Only one wall partially remained, the rest of the building a heap of blackened rubble. The whorehouse had become a tomb.

Then Foxy was climbing, finding footholds in the hexagonal wire and cresting the top of the fence. She landed on the other side, in the forbidden zone, and scurried into the shadows.

Among the ruins, all was quiet.

The lower portion of the staircase was visible against the remaining wall, and sadness welled within her. How many times had she climbed those stairs, an eager client following behind her? And how many of her old friends were buried beneath the debris, never to be recovered?

She walked among the destruction, choosing where to place her feet carefully. If she slipped and hurt herself, or got stuck, there was no one around to help her. Due to the sinister network of tunnels, the three-mile stretch from the cemetery to the brothel had been officially condemned as unsafe. People were evacuated from their homes, whole sections of the city cordoned off like the aftermath of a nuclear incident.

"I'm sorry I couldn't save you," she said to Candy, the words drifting away on the wind. "I hope you're in a better place now." The stitches under her ear itched, and she tried to scratch at them beneath the layers of bandages. The moon slipped behind a cloud, plunging the street into absolute darkness. No electricity had served the area since the disaster. She looked across the river at New Jersey, the twinkling lights reflected in the water, and decided to wait until the moon reappeared. She couldn't risk—

"What's that?" she whispered, as she spied a gentle, almost unnoticeable glow from deep within the ruins. A flashlight? No, it flickered like fire.

*Like fire...*

The light drew her towards it, and all at once she knew precisely where it was coming from. For where else would a furnace be, if not the basement? It couldn't still be operational, obviously. It was impossible. But then, a few weeks ago, it had rained blood and the dead had risen, so Foxy supposed nothing was ever off the cards in New York City.

She navigated her way through the rocks and broken planks and beams. Arriving at the source of the light, she found the old metal door lying flat across the ground. It looked in pretty good shape. She prised it up onto its side, then let go, the door toppling over and clanging loudly. Had anyone heard? No, of course not. The area was deserted.

She stared at the unblemished wooden staircase that led to the basement. The priest had survived down there, all those years ago, the firefighters locating him a full week after the church burned down. Martha had told her all about it, and while Martha was many things — greedy and cruel, for a start — she was most assuredly not a liar.

The furnace flickered in the darkness, and Foxy started down. The light grew brighter as she descended, the heat melting the snowflakes in her hair.

"My god," she said, as she reached the bottom of the stairs. The room had emerged from the blaze entirely unscathed, and looking exactly as it always had. Well... *almost*. Though the pews were stacked by the wall as usual, and the moldy cardboard boxes still threatened to topple at any moment, there was one key difference.

The life-size wooden crucifix.

It lay in the center of the basement, rather than leaning against the pews. And there was something else about it, too... something different. Foxy took a step closer, glancing over her shoulder to make sure... *what,* exactly? That no one had followed her in? That the building hadn't collapsed further, trapping her inside for eternity?

Everything was fine, and by the glow of the furnace, she looked down at the crucifix.

"Oh, fuck," she said.

She kneeled, heart racing, and laid her hands on the wooden figure.

"It can't be..."

The carving had changed. It was no longer in the image of Jesus Christ. Unless, of course, Jesus had a vagina, but Foxy didn't remember hearing about *that* in Sunday School. She ran her eyes from the carved wooden crotch to the small, delicately sculpted breasts, then settled on the face.

"Candy," she moaned softly, as she gazed into the contorted, grimacing visage of her friend. She inspected the sculpture with her hands, finding nothing but solid wood. She rapped her knuckles off it, a tear rolling down her cheek. It landed on the carving and was quickly absorbed.

Weeping, Foxy laid her head against Candy's chest. "What happened to you... what happened..."

Suddenly, she jerked away, her features warped with fear and confusion. What the fuck had she heard? It sounded like...

With great trepidation, she put her ear to the figure's chest once more, and listened.

A heartbeat.

It couldn't be...

Something creaked, the wood groaning like a ship battered by the waves. Foxy turned to see the carved fingers *moving*. The figure was alive! It wrenched one hand free from the nail as the mouth opened, emitting an unholy, tortured wail.

"Candy?" whispered Foxy. "Is that you?"

The wooden hand reached for the carving's face, pressing the fingers into the open mouth and pulling. The wood bent. It split. It cracked off in a large chunk, revealing pale pink flesh beneath.

"Oh my god, I thought you were gone," sobbed Foxy. She got unsteadily to her feet, leaning over, trying to get a better view of her friend.

But when she stared into the frenzied, maddening face of Father Patrick Morgan, she could do nothing but scream.

"It's a miracle!" spluttered the priest, blood spitting from his mouth and trailing down his chin. "It's a—"

Foxy's foot came down hard. Her winter boot smashed the priest's teeth and jaw, and when she raised it, the footwear was still connected to his face by a bloody trail of mucus.

He stared up at her with hatred burning in his eyes; hatred and contempt and lust and insanity.

"*Whore...*" he slurred. "*Jezebel... slut!*"

"Go to hell, motherfucker," said Foxy, and stomped her foot down again, obliterating his head.

This time, there was nothing left.

Foxy climbed wearily back up the stairs. Behind her, the cross burned. She had used her lighter and the last dregs of her vodka to set it on fire, then sparked up a joint from the flames. She watched for a while, making sure the priest was truly dead, then left the basement forever.

Outside, the snow fell heavily, coating the ruins in a soft white blanket. It crunched underfoot as Foxy crossed to the fence, leaving a trail of bloody prints. There, she clambered back over and started walking, though she wasn't sure where to. She just knew she needed to walk. As she ambled through the deserted streets, passing not a soul, she wondered what would happen to the Manhattan Riverfront Church site. Would a new structure be put up in its place? Probably. That was the nature of progress, after all.

"Give it some windows this time," she said to herself, her breath fogging before her eyes. She stuffed her hands in her pockets. "And leave the dead alone."

She walked all night, occasionally stopping in a doorway to shelter from the snow and have a smoke. She had nowhere to go, nowhere to be.

No home.

No friends.

No *family*.

All she *did* have were the clothes on her back and twelve dollars of change in her pocket. It wasn't much, she knew, but it was enough.

And as the sun rose on New York City, Foxy slipped into

a phone booth. There, she lit her last smoke, dropped a dime into the slot, and dialed, surprised she still remembered the number after everything she had been through.

The phone rang... and rang... and rang... and just when Foxy was about to give up, a woman answered.

"Mom?" said Foxy. "It's me. It's Rochelle." She paused, tears spilling down her cheeks. "Mom... I'm coming home."

# AFTERWORD

Thank you for reading *And By God's Hand You Shall Die*.

The story came about by chance one day when I was mucking about on Adobe Illustrator, the program I use to create my book covers. I was trying out different fonts, and needed a title to use, quickly deciding on the ridiculous *Haunted Brothel*. An hour later, I suddenly had the bare bones of a new story. Sometimes, that's all it takes.

It was intended as a loving homage to the blood-soaked, dream-logic horrors of the Italian Godfather of Gore, Lucio Fulci, and specifically his extraordinary run of masterpieces from *Zombi 2* and *City of the Living Dead* to *The Beyond* and *The House by the Cemetery*. If you enjoyed this story, I urge you to check those films out. A viewing of The Beyond on grotty bootleg VHS back in the 90s certainly changed my life, and I've never looked back.

~

As ever, I couldn't have written this book without the love

and support of my wife Heather and my best friend, the impossibly small and foolish Boris the pug.

I'm also very grateful to Ryan William Kay for his fantastic cover art.

And lastly, but most importantly, thank *you,* dear readers. Thank you from the bottom of my heart for taking a chance on truly independent horror. It's been a hell of a ride so far, and I promise you, there's *plenty* more to come.

Take it easy, friends.

This book was written to the music of Philip Glass.

# ABOUT THE AUTHOR

David Sodergren lives in Scotland with his wife Heather and his best friend, Boris the Pug.

Growing up, he was the kind of kid who collected rubber skeletons and lived for horror movies. Not much has changed since then.

His best known books include the gory and romantic fairy tale The Haar, the blood-drenched folk-horror Maggie's Grave, and the analog-horror fever dream Rotten Tommy. David also writes under the pseudonym Carl John Lee, publishing splatterpunk novels such as Psychic Teenage Bloodbath and Cannibal Vengeance.

instagram.com/paperbacksandpugs

# ALSO BY DAVID SODERGREN

The Forgotten Island

Night Shoot

Dead Girl Blues

Maggie's Grave

The Navajo Nightmare (with Steve Stred)

The Perfect Victim

Satan's Burnouts Must Die!

The Haar

And By God's Hand You Shall Die

Rotten Tommy

Summer of the Monsters

## Writing as Carl John Lee

The Blood Beast Mutations

Horror House of Perversion

Cannibal Vengeance

Horror House of Perversion 2: The Slaughtered Lambs

Psychic Teenage Bloodbath

Death Freaks on Hell's Highway

Psychic Teenage Bloodbath II